When **Kali Anthony** read her first romance novel at fourteen she realised two truths: that there can never be too many happy endings and that one day she would write them herself. After marrying her own tall, dark and handsome hero, in a perfect friends-to-lovers romance, Kali took the plunge and penned her first story. Writing has been a love affair ever since. If she isn't battling her cat for access to the keyboard, you can find Kali playing dress-up in vintage clothes, gardening, or bushwalking with her husband and three children in the rainforests of South-East Queensland.

This is Kali Anthony's debut book
for Mills & Boon Modern.
We hope that you enjoy it!

Discover more at millsandboon.co.uk.

REVELATIONS OF HIS RUNAWAY BRIDE

KALI ANTHONY

MILLS & BOON

First Published in Great Britain 2020
by Mills & Boon, an imprint of HarperCollins*Publishers*
1 London Bridge Street, London, SE1 9GF

© 2020 Kali Anthony

ISBN: 978-0-263-08863-2

MIX
Paper from
responsible sources
FSC™ C007454

This book is produced from independently certified FSC™ paper
to ensure responsible forest management.
For more information visit www.harpercollins.co.uk/green.

Printed and bound in Great Britain
by CPI Group (UK) Ltd, Croydon, CR0 4YY

FALKIRK COUNCIL LIBRARY

To my mother, Dot.
Wish you were here to enjoy the journey with me.
You'd have loved the ride.
Always in my heart.

CHAPTER ONE

THEA STRUGGLED IN the near darkness to tear free of the wedding dress she'd been forced to wear. The cursed laces of its bodice trussed her as tight as a chicken ready for roasting. She fumbled with the tangled bow at the small of her back, then stopped to steady her trembling fingers. Her breaths blew sharp and fast, and the cloying scent of citrus blossom from her bridal bouquet threatened to overwhelm her. No time for clumsiness. Tonight was about speed and execution. Because this plan—her only plan—allowed no room for failure.

'It's never going to work.'

Thea faced the quavering voice. Sheathed in soft cream silk, her best friend huddled in a shadowy corner. The brim of an oversized hat swooped across her face.

'We've been over this, Elena. It will.'

It has to.

There were no second chances. Outside, the hungry crowd and her husband waited. The man now entitled to all of her. Thea shuddered. He wouldn't get her mind, her body or her soul. This was her moment to escape. Tonight she'd break free and show them all.

'How do I look?'

Elena moved into what dim light shone through a lavishly curtained window from the dreary alleyway beyond. She smoothed her hands over the front of the dress, which swirled barely above her knees. Demure. Perfect. The dress Thea should be changing into now.

'Like more of a bride than I feel. Nobody will realise.'

Till it was too late. Till she was gone.

Everyone said she and Elena could pass as sisters, or as

each other. And they regularly did—with laughable ease. Allowing Thea a shred of freedom otherwise denied her.

Now all the years of planning her escape were over.

She walked to her friend and held her in a tight hug. Elena's body quaked in the embrace.

'Thank you. For this. For everything,' Thea said.

Elena returned the hug, then pushed away, wiping at her eyes. 'Let's get you out of that wedding dress and away from here.'

Thea turned and flinched as Elena's frantic hands fought the laces which bound her.

'Can we put on some lights?' Elena whispered. 'I can't see to do this quickly.'

'What if someone walks in? Like this, it's hard to tell who's who. Now, remember what I said?'

Elena laughed. There was nothing cheerful about the sound. 'Skirt the edges of the room. Keep the hat brim down. If anyone tries to talk to me pretend to cry and hide my face in a handkerchief like I'm overwrought by the sheer joy of this blessed marriage. Easy.'

One final pull and the bodice fell free. But Thea wasn't quite free yet. Her friend started on the laces of the corset.

'No time!' She wriggled away to search for the rest of her clothes. 'And it *will* work. We've told everyone about the hat and dress I'm wearing to leave here. People will be looking out for that, not for me.'

No one saw *her*. Sure, they saw her clothes, her jewels. Evidence of her father's money when he decided to show her off like some prize pony. That's why she and Elena were interchangeable. People were told about a sensational dress and hat and that was all they'd see—not the person wearing it.

Because to her father's friends she was nobody. A shadow who could slip away. And when somebody finally did notice, it would be too late.

'But Christo…'

Thea's heart dropped a beat at the sound of his name. She licked the perspiration beading on her top lip.

Christo Callas.

My husband.

No need for pretence now. Yet she'd slipped in those last moments. When Christo had lifted her veil. She'd looked into his unfathomable olive-tinged eyes and hadn't been able to quell the serpent inside. The knowledge that she'd been forced into this marriage to save her half-brother Alexis. Potent emotion had coiled and then reared, begging her to strike out at the man who'd effectively bought her. And in that moment he'd hesitated. As if he *knew.*

So she'd painted a sweet, soft smile on her face. Waited for the kiss which would transform her from Thea Lambros to Thea Callas. And, for all the horror of it, Christo's lips had been warm and soft with something that had felt like understanding…

No! She scrubbed at her mouth, smearing the shell-pink lipstick. Wiping away the strange tingling the memory had wrought.

'Thea?'

'Christo won't notice either.'

He didn't understand her—hadn't even tried.

Thea thrust Elena the bridal bouquet which had lain wilting on a side table.

'He's not interested in me—only in what this marriage can do for him. One woman's the same as another to men like that.'

To Christo she was simply a commodity. Like she was to her father, who'd made it clear she must agree to the marriage as part of a business deal. If she didn't, Alexis would go to jail.

But now, with Alexis's freedom bought, she could run. Extract herself from whatever questionable scheme her father had concocted. Her plan all along.

'I hope you're right,' Elena said.

There was no time for doubts now. Thea stepped out of her dress and flung it into a dark corner, where it flopped like a discarded marshmallow. The suffocating corset could wait till she was safely hidden. She'd cut the damn thing off if she had to.

'I fit the job description,' she said, pulling on a practical black knit top. 'A compliant bed-warmer.'

Her blood ran hot with a furious roar. She knew her own worth—and it was *not* playing that role. Not for any man.

Thea shrugged into a heavy leather jacket, then zipped and buckled the front. Earlier she'd hidden her jeans and boots under the ridiculous confection of a dress now deflating in the corner.

It was almost time to go.

Thea walked to Elena and took her hands. The chill of them shivered through her. 'Are you sure you'll be okay?' She squeezed Elena's fingers in reassurance. 'I'm not asking too much?'

Elena squeezed back. 'You're like my sister. What wouldn't I do for you? And I can look after myself. Time to live your life. You've been caged long enough.'

In the Lambros family cage.

For most of her twenty-three years she'd only known one sibling. Demetri. A cruel thug disguised in civilised clothes. He'd always been her father's enforcer, and Thea his first victim. Her father hadn't cared. Not about the little girl who looked too much like her mother. The wife who'd had the temerity to leave him.

No. Thea never wished to set eyes on Demetri or her father again. But Alexis...

She pulled her phone from the pocket of her jeans. From the moment he'd inveigled himself into their home as her bodyguard two years earlier things had become almost bearable. His presence had kept her going. But since this morning he hadn't responded to her texts.

Elena frowned as Thea checked her phone. 'Still no word?'

'Nothing… But it'll be okay.'

Thea chewed her bottom lip till she tasted the tang of blood. Surely he'd left Athens? She rubbed at the ache in her chest. The pain of having to leave him so soon ran soul-deep. Only the knowledge that her marriage had freed him kept her going.

She took a shuddering breath. 'And when you're discovered?'

Because Elena would be—it was only a matter of time. But everyone had to believe what they were told so they'd search in the wrong place.

'Where have I gone?'

'You've taken a hire car.' Elena's bottom lip quivered. Her eyes brimmed with the glitter of tears as she played her role with breathless innocence and trembling perfection. 'You're driving towards Karpathos. To visit your mother's grave.'

Thea had wanted to go before the wedding. Her father had refused to allow it. Try as he might, he'd never excised her mother's memory from her life, so her visiting there would make sense to him. It was a subtle mix of truth and fiction blended into a believable enough concoction.

Still. It didn't feel right.

'I hate using Mama's memory this way.'

Elena shook her head. 'Maria would have approved. Anything to get you away from men like those. But forget that. Was I good enough?'

'You should become an actress,' Thea said. 'After that flawless performance Christo's minions will definitely head south looking for me.'

'And you'll be starting your new life.' Elena smiled—her first display of happiness on this bleak day. 'Can't you tell me where you're going?'

'No. It's safer this way.' It would protect Elena as much as herself in the little time they had.

Thea grabbed her motorcycle helmet from the chair behind her, hesitating.

'How in Hades am I going to get this over my stupid hair?'

All that teasing and plaiting... The style had taken aeons to create, with the hairdresser cooing over what would be a wasted effort.

Elena pulled at a few of the sculpted curls. 'It'll take an hour to get rid of these pins!'

'No time for that. I'll squash the helmet over the top somehow. How much time have we spent already?'

Elena checked her watch. 'We haven't been long. Anyhow, they're too busy drinking your father's ouzo to care. Everyone's going to think you're spending ages to look beautiful for Christo. And once you leave they'll have to go—which none of them want.'

It was the sad truth. Thea had no idea who most of the people at the wedding were. Business associates, she suspected. More deals and alliances being sealed over the carcass of her blighted union. Vultures, the lot of them. They were interested in the food, the alcohol, *the spectacle.*

'I'll never forget what you did for me. When it's safe, I'll try to let you know where...'

Thea swallowed the lump tightening her throat. There were few people she loved. Elena. Alexis. The thought of leaving them crushed her.

Elena waved her away. 'I'm holding you to that. One day when we're both grandmothers we'll drink coffee together and laugh about today,' she said, searching through a bag, then thrusting Thea an envelope. 'Don't forget this. Passport. Money. Bank details. It's all there. Now, go! Be happy.'

Thea hesitated. She slipped her hand into her jacket pocket and rubbed the worn St Christopher medal on its fine chain, safely nestled there. Then she grabbed her padded gloves and secreted rucksack, moving to slip out of the door at the back of the room, which led to the alley where her motorcycle was hidden.

The door was usually kept locked, but she'd been able to charm the manager of the venue into leaving it unsecured for a fictional delivery. *A surprise for the groom.*

'Wait!' Elena squeaked.

Thea whipped around, her heart pounding with the electric spike of adrenalin. They'd been discovered?

All she saw was her friend, a slender shape framed by the light from the doorway behind.

'What?'

'Rings!'

How could she have forgotten her engagement ring? The dead weight of the baguette diamond. Huge. Impossible to miss. And her wedding ring wasn't far behind, with its twinkling encrustation of pure white gemstones. Her husband's mark. His claim.

Thea prised the pair of them from her finger and handed them to her friend. *Now* she was free.

Time to go.

'And that is where this absurd charade ends.'

The deep, growling voice rumbled like thunder as a shadow loomed from a darkened alcove.

Christo.

Christo strolled over to a petite side table and turned on a lamp. The room shone with a soft glow. Such a pretty space, with delicate gilt furniture and swathes of brocade fabric draping the walls. Perfect for wedding preparations. Not so perfect for the curious machinations of the two wide-eyed females now frozen before him.

He'd been prepared to allow their odd scene to take its course. There was no chance of his sparkling new bride running away. One of his men stood waiting outside the door. She would have walked into a wall of immovable security.

He gritted his teeth. Breathed through the heat blistering his veins. *The rings.*

Holding out his hand, he nodded to the Drakos girl. She placed Thea's bouquet on one of the fine chairs and dropped the glittering tokens into his palm. He curled them into his fist and they burned in his hand. Hundreds of thousands of euros in jewellery sat there, abandoned without care.

Christo slid them into the pocket of his trousers and addressed Thea's bridesmaid. 'Leave us.' He kept his voice level and calm. His bride and his future were secure for now. Any further emotion was misdirected.

'You can't make me. I'm staying here.'

Such a brave statement. Christo smiled. He'd been told he looked wolf-like when he did, so he tried for a less predatory edge. Elena shuddered, and wilted a fraction. Ah, so he'd failed. Again.

He sighed, reaching into his pocket for his phone. Pressed speed dial. 'Raul,' he said evenly, 'I need you. Miss Drakos would like to dance.'

He'd attend to Thea soon enough. From the corner of his eye he glimpsed her, standing straight. Stiff. Glancing at the door. Would she run or hold her ground? He suspected the former and hoped for the latter. Why? It was hard to say. He was used to women running when life didn't meet their expectations. His mother had been the finest advocate of *that* coping strategy.

Raul, his appointed head of security and best man, arrived at the door. Elena was the maid of honour. She was required to dance with Raul at some point. Now was an opportune time as any.

'Elena stays.'

The lady speaks. Although it was more like a hiss. Quiet. Serpentine. Curling a chill tight on his spine.

He ignored it. 'Elena, you'll dance with Raul *now.*'

Christo had little doubt she'd leave. His commands were invariably followed. Raul held out his hand. His prospective dance partner took it, removed her ridiculous hat, placed it on a chair and left the room with a tearful *'Sorry...'* to Christo's bride. Such a touching moment.

He turned his attention to Thea.

She didn't wilt. She stood rigid. Head held high. So fierce and proud. Dressed in jeans and leather with exquisitely coiffed and braided hair. All contradiction—such a heady mix.

A tantalising buzz thrummed through him.

'How long were you hiding there?' she asked.

Christo would allow her some questions. He had a lifetime to get answers of his own.

'Long enough.'

'And you watched us dress?'

He shrugged. 'There was nothing to see.'

She'd been half dressed already. Yet even in the darkened room Thea had blinded him. Her gentle curves. The slender waist. That crushing corset. An interesting foil for jeans and heavy boots... Everything about her had proved interesting tonight.

'I didn't realise my husband *lurked.* I would never have married you if I'd known. Lurkers can't be trusted.'

He laughed. Such an unfamiliar thing it sounded more like a bark. Thea didn't flinch. Most people would have.

'That's something I've never been accused of. I'll add it to the list of my many documented achievements.'

His laughter seemed to increase her courage. She took a step forward. Still clutching her gloves, helmet and a white envelope. He wanted that envelope.

Instead of taking it, as he would in due course, Christo allowed her another question. He knew it was coming. Her brows creased in a slight frown and her mouth was opening and closing a fraction, as if silently practising the words.

'How did you find out?'

Her voice stroked soft as a feather over his skin. The perfect balance of seduction and wheedling. Lashes downcast. Deferential. If she'd been close enough no doubt she'd have placed a fine-boned hand on his. Gazed into his eyes. Perhaps granted him a few false tears. Such a subtle act, and all too familiar.

He despised it.

'Take care, Thea. I don't endure theatrics.'

She tossed her head and the artfully placed curls of her hair flicked and bounced. 'I'm no performing seal.'

'Then what's today been about, if not a performance?'

He'd known she had spark. That much had been evident in the interminable parades he suspected her father had imposed upon her each time Christo had visited their ostentatious home. Thea's beauty shone fierce and bright, and such beauty came from intelligence. Yet she'd attempted to hide it from him until today.

When he'd lifted her veil there it had been, boiling through her icy veneer. Those eyes...tight and burning with hatred. He'd almost recoiled, witnessing the wild creature beneath. And then her face had smoothed, as if a wave had washed away writing on sand, and it had gone.

But he'd watched her at the reception. She and her friend wandering to and from this room. The furtive whispers between them. After one trip Thea's skirt had hung more loosely. After another the hem had dragged on the floor. So he'd schooled Raul, had the door to the alley placed under guard and silently thwarted her plans.

Creeping into this room to wait in the darkness was beneath him, perhaps. Still, he'd needed to witness the deception personally. It would serve as a reminder of why he couldn't trust.

Thea hadn't taken long to reveal herself.

'Today? It was about escaping *you*.'

The words might sting, but he was used to his parents' rejection so what did one more matter? He'd been the child they'd weaponised to hurt each other, not loved for being their son. That was what the people closest to you were capable of.

He'd inured himself against the pain of those boyhood lessons years ago. Never again would he beg for meagre crumbs of affection from another's table. All he dealt in now were cold truths and hard cash. And Atlas Shipping, the company his grandfather had founded, was his ultimate and only reward for being born into the misery of his family.

Christo walked towards Thea, towering above her. At six foot four, he towered above most people. It was an edge which many might exploit, but he refused to be known as a bully.

He rolled his tight shoulders. Swallowed down the anger roiling in his gut. Tried again for a smile which was conciliatory. Who knew whether it had worked? As she looked up at him Thea's face was as blank as a fresh sheet of paper.

'You want an escape, and yet I still have you.'

Christo plucked the envelope from her hand and slid it into the inner pocket of his tuxedo. Thea wasn't expecting it. She broke a little. A slump of her shoulders. A tremble in her bottom lip. Her freedom had been stolen, as his had been.

Would she understand? He almost felt sorry for her in that moment, but finer feelings had no place here. Later he might make time to regret what he had to do. Not tonight.

'Wait. I can't… I won't…'

Emotion ran high in her voice as it quavered and cracked. Nothing moved him. He had no choice. She'd realise soon enough and then a deal could be struck—although only on his terms, because her compliance was essential.

'Did you really think your childish plan would work?' He schooled his voice, low and sharp as a blade. He'd witnessed grown men crumble at this tone. 'That I wouldn't notice the switch immediately with only that monstrosity of a headpiece as a disguise?' He nodded to the discarded hat.

She dropped her helmet and gloves onto a chair. Brushed

a fine strand of hair behind her ear. 'It was all about mis-direction.'

'So now you're playing conjuror's tricks?'

'I was supposed to be a happy, blushing bride—not a prisoner planning an escape. People saw what they wanted to.'

Well, her confidence was misplaced. Time to show her.

He cupped her chin in his right hand, felt Thea's perfect skin, silky and warm under his fingers. Her lips thinned, but she didn't move.

'I see your cognac eyes. Your skin like mountain honey. And your hair rich as dark chocolate,' he said, his voice pitched soft as a caress. 'I see your haughty grace as you walk. The ferocity in your gaze. I see who you try to hide. I see *you*, Thea.'

A new look flickered across her face. *That* look he understood. Those incendiary eyes were all flash and fire. He wanted to set her alight and watch her burn. But he wouldn't. He wasn't weak, like his father. Falling for lies about love. Letting a woman trap him into marriage. Love was for vulnerable fools. Not him. Having once been a weapon, he'd learned how to defend himself. And love was the deadliest weapon of them all.

Yet as he looked down at her, Thea's glorious lips parted. Her pupils went dark and wide. So he dropped his head and brushed his lips across hers as a test. For effect. She gasped when he pulled away.

'Elena is a pretty dark-haired, brown-eyed girl,' he said, his lips burning where they'd touched hers. 'But she could *never* pass as you. You're a fool to imagine it.'

He released this new Thea. This aware Thea.

She raised shaking fingers to her lips. He took her free hand, dropped the rings back into it. She snatched her hand away and looked down at them, eyes still wide. Not so good at hiding now. Her mouth fell open, her skin paling to ivory.

He knew that look too. Horror.

His stomach clenched. He'd felt much the same when he'd realised he required a bride. A cruel trick of his father's. Christo had sworn off marriage until Hector's actions made it necessary. His father had procured secret loans from Thea's. Failed to pay the crippling interest. Become indebted to a man who had demanded Christo's marriage to his daughter to stop the impending foreclosure.

Christo didn't want this debacle any more than Thea did. Still, no matter how distasteful the task, he'd do whatever was required to save Atlas Shipping. To secure his birthright, his inheritance and the company his father had nearly destroyed.

'It would have worked,' Thea whispered. 'It *would* have.'

'Perhaps if you'd married anyone else. Unfortunately, you married me.'

Thea's hand clenched into a fist, tight around the rings. 'And what's so special about you?'

'I understand people.' He'd learned as a child. So he knew when to hide from his hostile mother. To avoid his mercurial father. For Christo, people were transparent as glass. 'It's why I'm unparalleled in business.'

'I'd say you have an unparalleled ego.'

He stalked past Thea and opened the rear door of the room. The gritty smell of real life wafted in from the alley behind. He spoke to the man outside and ordered him in.

'An ego's only worth something if it's backed by ability. Which I have. You see, Thea, your plan *wouldn't* have worked.' He stood back and let her take in the hulking security guard he'd posted outside. 'There was no chance you'd escape. Every exit was being watched. Your transportation is now safely in my garage. You'd failed even before you'd begun. Accept it.'

He nodded to his man, who left the room. Thea watched him go, realisation spreading across her face.

'I'm not a slave to be traded. I won't stay with you. This marriage is a sham.'

In some ways, he agreed with her. Yet here he stood, with a gold wedding band prickling on his finger. Thea still held her rings. He needed her to put them on. If she did, he'd won—for tonight.

'You're asking me to return you to the tender care of your father?' A man Christo suspected didn't have a sentimental, loving bone in his body.

Thea grabbed the back of a spindly chair, clutching it till her fingers blanched. 'I'm asking you to let me go.'

'No.'

Christo had heard whispers about Tito Lambros. He was reported to be cruel and vindictive. The bitter burn of loathing coursed like poison through his veins. That his father's negligence had allowed such a man to hold Christo's future in his hands…

There was a great deal he needed to learn about Thea's family—some of which he might be able to use. But that could wait. Now it was time to give her something to cling to. *Hope.*

'You'll come with me as my wife and we'll discuss the situation in which we find ourselves. That's my promise. But we're leaving now.'

She looked down at her clothes and back at him. Her liquid amber eyes glowed in the soft lights. 'I can't go dressed like this!'

No more delays. She glanced at the door again. He didn't want a scene. Her tantrums could occur at his home, where any witnesses would be paid to hold their silence.

'You look perfect,' he said, waving his hand in her direction. 'It shows a flair for the dramatic—which you've proved to have in abundance tonight. Our exit will be unforgettable.'

She seemed to compose herself. Thrust her chin high, all glorious defiance. 'But my hat… I told everyone about it. I can't disappoint them.'

'Life's full of disappointments. Tell them it wouldn't fit over your magnificent hair.'

Thea's lips twitched in a barely suppressed sneer, her eyes narrow and glacial. The look she threw him would have slayed a mere mortal. Luckily for the most part he felt barely human.

'Rings,' he said.

She jammed them carelessly on her finger. *Victory.* He held out the crook of his arm and she hesitated before slipping hers through it. All stiff and severe. But her body still fitted into his in a way which enticed him. Caused his heart to thrum, his blood to roar. Strange. Intoxicating. All Thea.

'Now, smile,' he said.

She plastered on a mocking grimace.

He leaned down and whispered in her ear. 'Like you mean it, *koukla mou.*'

'I'll smile when you say *that* like you mean it, Christo.'

And he laughed.

This second laugh was more practised. More familiar—like an old memory. But the warmth growing in his chest was real. Beyond all expectations, he was enjoying her. For his sanity, perhaps a little too much...

CHAPTER TWO

THEA TUCKED INTO a corner of the limousine, far away from her newly minted husband. No one had noticed her biker chic clothes as they'd left the reception venue. They hadn't paid much attention to her at all. Everyone had been congratulating Christo. Shaking his hand. Wishing him happiness. The only tears for her had been shed by Elena.

Thea didn't have time for tears. She had to pull herself together. Devise another plan. Her focus needed to be on the future—which now sat in a white envelope in the pocket of Christo's jacket.

But how to get it?

She looked over at him. His long, lean legs stretched out, relaxed. His face illuminated by the cool glow of his phone. Some might call him handsome. Incredibly so, with his regal nose, strong jaw and high-cut cheekbones, all cast in a way to make a sculptor swoon. She, on the other hand, loathed the sight of his testosterone-fuelled perfection.

Though seduction might work… It was their wedding night, after all. She could try. Croon something…she wasn't sure what…slip a hand beneath his jacket, kiss him…

Christo's mouth formed a disapproving line as he tapped at his phone. She'd already had a taste of that mouth. The soft, chaste kiss at the altar. That shocking moment when he'd brushed his lips against hers at the reception venue and they'd sparked as if touched by a live wire.

She lifted her hand to her mouth, which still tingled.

Even if she could grab the envelope at the perfect moment, what then? She shook her head. A few grains of rice clattered from her hair onto the leather seats. The element of surprise was gone, so she couldn't try that approach. There must be something else.

Christo turned to peer at her. One eye was shadowed in darkness. The blue light from his phone turning the other inhumanly green. The effect made him look something like a pirate.

There was no way she was going to let him plunder *her* treasures. Her fresh plans started now.

'Where are we going?'

'Home.'

'No honeymoon? Christo Callas—ever the romantic,' she said, placing a hand to her heart. 'I'm *so* lucky.'

'You want romance?' He raised an eyebrow. 'You're the one who pronounced our marriage a sham. Had you not, we'd have been on our way to a week of wedded bliss on my island.'

An island? Typical. Though, come to think of it, not even her father had one of those. 'You had to cancel? How inconvenient.'

'For my staff, perhaps. Though I admit standing down the jet *was* an irritation.'

Something about being the cause of one of his irritations irked her. 'So…what? If I'd been a good girl, in exchange for my freedom I'd have been rewarded with a joy-ride and some time at the beach? Lucky me. Would you have supplied chocolate mints on my pillow too?'

He wasn't looking at her now. Instead he studied the dull glow of the city, which washed his imposing form with gold light. The breath caught in her throat. For a moment she forgot who he was, transfixed by the beauty of the picture.

'An island in the Echinades, a home in the mountains, a yacht berthed in…' he opened the calendar on his phone and checked something '… Monaco and an apartment in New York—any of which you could have flown to in my jet. And that's amongst other things. The rewards are many and varied for a *good* girl, as you put it.'

Thea had come from wealth—though nothing like this. She and Elena had discussed it when her father had made terrifyingly clear she had to marry to prevent Alexis rotting in a jail cell. They'd talked about Thea enjoying the considerable fruits of Christo's fortune.

Could she do it now? Christo would spend his days in the city, working. She could go anywhere. New York? That was where her mother had promised to take her all those years ago. Before she'd died, when life had held some hope. She'd like New York, she supposed.

And then came the reality of the price she'd have to pay. Because there was always a price. Her body was the currency of this union.

Never.

'I'm not prostituting myself for a chance to dip my toes in the Aegean or for a ride on your boat!'

'Yacht. Crewed by forty. And that's what marriage is about. Fair exchange for services rendered.'

Yes, marriage was a cruel snare. She'd seen it imprison her mother, and other women too. The wives of her father's friends. Locked in gilded cages where they fawned and simpered for attention from callous men. She'd planned never to be fooled by that trap, no matter how cunningly laid. The lure of money or circumstance...or love would never bind her to another...

'So cynical,' said Christo. 'On your wedding day too. You could have refused the offer at any time until we were pronounced man and wife. Yet here we are.'

'*Offer?* You never *asked* me to marry. I was an afterthought. You and my father negotiated the terms of my servitude. One day I woke up engaged and was thrown a ring in a box. Stop trying to turn this into some grand sacrifice on your part.'

'Don't presume to know *anything* about my sacrifices!'

Christo's words snapped like a whip-crack. Thea couldn't see his face, shrouded in darkness as they were. But the cut of his voice carved right to her soul.

'I was informed that you were satisfied with the arrangement. So you wanted a man on bended knee, professing love and adoration? If I'd done that what would your answer have been?'

Thea dropped her head, toying with the wedding and engagement rings which itched and burned her finger. She'd refused her father's demands to marry at first, and so he'd cut off any meagre freedoms she'd still had.

Demetri's methods of persuasion had been more brutal. The twin threats of social seclusion and physical force usually ensured her compliance, but she'd become braver since Alexis had entered her home. That day he'd stepped in to protect her had changed everything.

Her father then realised his importance to Thea. Not only as her bodyguard, but her half-brother. He knew she'd do anything to save him—the love child her mother had been forced to give up before entering a loveless marriage.

She wrapped her arms round her waist. Closed her eyes.

'As I thought,' Christo said. 'You're having a tantrum because I didn't play Prince Charming.'

'You can think what you like.'

'I invariably do.'

She turned to look out at a world which had always passed her by. 'I don't care. Your good opinion of me doesn't matter.'

Self-recrimination ran riot through her head. She should have run earlier. But when Alexis had confessed who he was, everything had changed. He'd told her of the promises he'd made to protect Thea if their mother couldn't and each day had become a little more tolerable. So she'd stayed. Worked to ensure her future so she would be able to do more than eke out an impoverished existence like her mother had.

Yet when it had almost been time to leave, fate intervened. With Alexis paying the price for her cowardice.

She slumped in the seat.

'Perhaps you should learn to cultivate a friendly benefactor,' Christo said. 'It could make your life easier.'

She adjusted one of the loathsome hairpins, now pricking into her scalp. 'There's no vacancy for the role of friendly benefactor in my life.'

'Shame. If there was, I'd be available to fill it.'

Something had shifted his tone. Now there was a lightness. Was he entertained by this?

She looked over at him, and even in the dim light of the cabin she glimpsed the hint of a smirk. She wouldn't be baited.

'Since you're more *unsociable detractor*, fortunately you don't meet the job description.'

'I'm known to be extremely affable in the right circumstances.'

The car's interior closed in on her. She needed to get out of here.

Breathe. She must stay calm.

But how? In this claustrophobic space? Drowning in the scent of Christo?

It was something more than expensive cologne. A dark, intoxicating essence whispering of wild places. Of powerful, untamed male.

Thea shivered. Clenched her fists till the nails bit into her palms. She could *do* this. Christo had promised they'd talk. She'd hold him to it.

The car drove up to a wrought-iron gateway which slid open before it. As the vehicle slowed to a halt outside the front entrance of Christo's mansion Thea moved to open the door. Escape the confines of this space threatening to crush her.

'Stop,' Christo said.

She did—without thinking. His voice, quiet as a whisper on the breeze, had carried such force she knew he wasn't someone she could trifle with. She must make no mistake. Whatever liberties she took, it would only be those that he allowed her to take.

'You will play your part as a happy new bride. Even if...'

His eyes traced a path from her head to her toes and back again. Everywhere his gaze touched ignited in a flare of heat.

'Even if you don't look like one. Freedom is bought. You start paying now.'

Christo didn't wait for the driver. He exited the limo, bending down to hold out his hand for hers.

She looked at it for a heartbeat. Long, elegant fingers. Square, perfect nails. The shiny wedding ring that caught the light and glinted. She placed her hand in his. Warm, strong. Curling possessively around hers.

A strange feeling wove through their connected fingers. A sinuous tempting thing that whispered to her, heated her cheeks, made her pulse thready and panicked. There was power in his touch. And the sense of possession was overwhelming as he squeezed gently.

Snakes of fear uncurled in her belly. Slithering. Contorting. Knotting into one another. She couldn't take her eyes from the place where he held her tight. Held her prisoner. Would he ever let her go?

'Now look at me.'

She couldn't resist. His voice was like the sprinkle of rain on a summer's day, the breath of a warm breeze. Then there was his stillness. It terrified her more than any lashes of emotion.

'*Not* like that.' He frowned.

'Like what?'

'Like I'm a Cyclops,' he said. 'I want you to look at me in a way that tells everyone what you crave is a locked door, a big bed and me inside you for hours.'

His words cut off her breath as surely as if he'd grabbed her by the throat. She tore her hand free of his, almost crawling back into the car as she did so.

'I can play my part, but I'll never look at you like that.'

He raised one mocking eyebrow. 'Afraid you might like it?'

'Enough!'

She was no coward. Thea slid out of the limo. Stood. Waited for a moment to suck at the air before Christo placed a heated palm on the small of her back. And then she allowed herself to be escorted through the monolithic front doors to where a line-up of staff waited.

'Let's get this over with,' she said.

His home was a vast display of modern, elegant lines in whites, golds and blues. Though she didn't have much time to survey the place as Christo swept through it like a tidal surge.

He introduced her to each staff member by name. All of them were eager to meet the new Mrs Callas, but they slid by in a blur as he led her up a winding staircase, past artwork bursting from white walls.

Yet she couldn't take her mind from Christo's hand at the base of her spine. Strong. Possessive. She supposed it was meant to appear affectionate, but the staff had long ceased watching and had melted away as if they were ghosts. There was no need for it now.

'Where's my bag? My phone?' Thea asked, trying to take her mind off the burn of his palm.

She'd hardly brought anything with her—only enough to maintain the ruse.

'I have your phone. Your bag's being unpacked together with all your other possessions, which the removal company delivered this morning.'

Yet again she hadn't been consulted. Choking bile rose in her throat. There was nothing at her father's she wanted. Her life was meant to be starting elsewhere. Fresh, clean. Something she could create for herself, not borrow from others.

'How efficient. And unnecessary. I won't be here long.'

'You'll be here as long as I need you.'

His voice was all quiet intent. They were deep in the house now. Away from everyone—especially prying eyes.

'That's something we need to discuss,' she said.

He looked down upon her. Cold. Unreachable. Her heart slammed into her ribs.

'And we will.'

'Where?' she asked as they stopped before a set of double doors.

Christo turned the handles and thrust them open. 'In the bedroom, *koukla mou*.'

'I'm not sleeping with you!'

Her words were a breathy gasp as she stopped, rocking back on her feet.

Christo ignored her and strode inside, a hot burst of irritation running through him. What was she thinking? He'd never force himself on her.

Her presumption that he would made him reckless.

'Really, Thea? It *is* our wedding night. That's what newly married couples do.'

He turned. Thea was frozen like a statue on the threshold of his room. Eyes wide. Surveying him up and down.

'This isn't a real marriage. It was arranged.'

'Marriages are "arranged" for people like us all the time. This could be a real marriage.' Or as real as possible for someone in their position.

He'd anticipated a relationship with no passion. A performance of duty for them both. But a lack of passion was not something he could imagine now. This new Thea intrigued him. His heart throbbed with a curious rhythm, as if charged with a fresh energy.

What he'd been promised by Tito Lambros, when Christo had realised the position his father had forced him into, was a sweet, obedient, chaste girl. He didn't hold much value in chastity. Better a woman who knew what she was doing, in his opinion. So he'd steeled himself for a wedding night of tutelage. The sweet and obedient type didn't thrill him either, but she would make a trouble-free sort of wife.

The woman in front of him was another creature altogether. One he didn't recognise from the quiet investigations he'd asked Raul to conduct, to ensure there was at least a modicum of truth behind her father's words.

He needed to check the work Raul had been asked to do.

'This can't be a real marriage. It'll never be consummated.'

Christo reached for a phone in the corner of the room and called the kitchens. 'Cognac. Two glasses, please.'

He shrugged off his jacket, cast it onto the chair next to him and tugged at his bow tie, letting it hang loose.

Thea hadn't moved, still standing in the doorway.

He undid the shirt button at his throat. Her gaze lowered, watching the flick of his fingers.

He undid the next. And the next. Then he stopped.

Her eyes hesitated at the open shirt showing part of his chest. As they burned on him with that strange heat, a crackling tension tightened in his gut.

'Come in. Close the door. Sit.'

A small flush whispered across Thea's cheeks and was gone. She looked away.

His stomach clenched at the loss of her eyes on his body. It was too much like disappointment. He ignored the sensation, removing his phone from his trouser pocket and tossing it on a table before sprawling on a plump couch.

His bedroom was more of a suite—the size of a small apartment and the one place in his home where he was rarely disturbed. They were safe here, for whatever histrionics were about to come.

He motioned to an armchair on the opposite side of an occasional table.

'I'm not your lap dog.'

'No, a lap dog would be less trouble. And it would at least jump all over me and be happy when I came home.'

She perched on the edge of the chair and glared at him as if she had murder on her mind.

A quiet knock at the door disturbed the uneasy silence.

A young woman in a crisp black uniform entered, carrying a silver tray.

'Thank you, Anna,' Christo said. 'Please leave the bottle.'

He suspected at least one of them might need fortifying for the negotiations to come.

The young woman placed the drinks on the table between them. 'Congratulations again, Mr and Mrs Callas. It's a happy day for you both.'

He tried to appear as pleased as his staff were. 'You have no idea…'

'Will that be all?'

Christo nodded.

Anna smiled at Thea and left the room.

He picked up one of the brandy balloons and swirled the glass in the light. Amber liquid coated the glass in a slick film of gold.

'A toast,' he said.

'What is it?'

Thea took a glass and sniffed it, wrinkling her nose. There was an unexpected cuteness about her when she did so. He smiled.

'Cognac.' Christo took a sip. Enjoyed the burn. The same type of burn as Thea's gaze upon him now. 'The colour of your eyes.'

She stopped and cocked her head. There was something so cool and unreachable about her. Yet her ferocity shone through. Those eyes of hers, spitting golden fire. The need to witness more of it, to experience her and the wildness she hid, grabbed him in a breath-stealing grip.

He hadn't expected to feel this way. The natural desire from contemplating a night with a beautiful woman, yes. Not this consuming sensation which thrummed through his every nerve, making him heavy and tight with lust for a woman he couldn't touch.

Thea placed the glass on the table without tasting it and slid it towards him. 'I've nothing to toast.'

'Shame… It's twenty-five years old. Obviously more mature than you.'

'I'm not the one being childish. I'm not the one playing games.'

She still refused to accept her part in the position where they now found themselves. 'Yes, Thea. You are. You've been playing games with me since the beginning and now I want answers.'

She leaned back into the armchair, feigning disinterest. But he could see by the tense set of her shoulders and the way her bottom lip puckered as she chewed at the inside that she was deeply concerned about what was happening here.

He reached over to his jacket, slung on the chair, and pulled out the white envelope. It might well have been a glass of water for someone parched in the desert the way Thea watched it, with a desperate craving stare.

Christo slid his thumbnail to unseal it. Made a show of inspecting the contents. Two thousand US dollars. Not so much. Certainly not enough for an escape. A passport. Nothing unusual there.

He unfolded a white piece of paper with account numbers written on it.

'Who taught you to ride a motorcycle?' he asked.

Her eyes widened a fraction. She hadn't been expecting that question, he was sure of it. Which had been his intention all along.

Thea licked her lips. They shone moist and pink. 'M-my brother… Demetri.'

Her brother was a dissolute, soft, rich boy, who only knew how to drive so he could show off his newest supercar. The thought that he could ride a motorcycle was absurd.

He let her lie sit unanswered, for now, and returned his attention to the paper in his hands.

'What bank is this?'

Thea crossed her arms.

'How much money is in the account?'

The silence stretched till it was thin and fragile. He waited.

When the thread was so thin Christo thought it would snap, Thea spoke. A low hiss, but he heard it nonetheless.

'That's none of your business.'

'You're my wife. Everything about you is my business. We can treat this…' he waved the paper about '…as your dowry.'

'No!'

He didn't need her money. The gift her father had granted him, halting the foreclosure, was greater than any paltry amount she no doubt held. But this was a battle he'd win. Her antics wouldn't put Atlas Shipping at risk. Not in the company's seventy-fifth year. It was a year for celebration, not failure. He'd never allow it. *Never.*

'One call to my personal banker and I'll have not only the name of your bank, but the balance of your account transferred into mine and secure.'

Thea twisted her small, delicate hands in her lap. 'You can't…'

'He was at the wedding,' Christo said, picking up his phone. 'All I need to say is that you've forgotten the details and want me to take care of it. Would you like me to get him now? No matter the time, he'll take my call.'

She looked at him. Eyes narrow, lips thin. Hatred evident. Once, long ago, he might have cared. Tonight, he didn't.

'Four million.'

He put down the sheet of paper. Leaned forward. He couldn't have heard properly.

'How much?'

'Four million US dollars or thereabouts.'

She lounged back in the chair looking like the fox who'd stolen a prized chicken. How had she accumulated that kind of money? Tito Lambros was known for being stingy. A banker who made money through frugality and question-able practices.

'Your father gave it to you?'

She snorted, before catching herself. There was his answer. Tito Lambros would never have given his daughter those sorts of funds. She must have stolen it, somehow.

'I'm thrifty.'

'Or a criminal. Should I ask your father to check his accounts? Perform an audit to look for a missing four million "or thereabouts"?'

When she spoke it was with pure derision. 'I'm no thief.'

'So what *is* my beautiful new wife? Not thrifty… Your clothes and shoes are exclusive designer.' He should know—he'd spent enough on former lovers to understand that much. 'Unless you've acquired a goose capable of laying golden eggs or the touch of Midas?'

The twitch of a smile played at the corner of her mouth. She was dying to tell him how she'd done it, so he let the statement linger. He needed to know how she'd acquired her money. It would inform what he did next, because he was beginning to watch Thea *very* closely.

Thea crossed her legs, wrapped her hands around her knee and studied him. He could see the thoughts behind her golden, intelligent eyes. She was calculating. Weighing up her options.

'My clothes and shoes were all given to me by Elena when she'd finished with them.'

'Then where—'

'In exchange for letting you know, I want something in return. To discuss our short and unfriendly future together.'

Negotiation was something he understood all too well. His parents had never offered him anything out of affection, but out of anticipation that they'd receive something in return. *Him*—a convenient tool in their hostilities. His inevitable conclusion? They didn't love him. They used him.

He'd become an expert on navigating that kind of emotional quicksand. And, with Thea, he'd get his own way. Still, he was prepared to allow her to think she might win.

'We'll discuss our options after you answer my question.'

She raised her eyebrows. 'That's meant to be my incentive? You'll have to give me something more than a promise.'

Thea sat straight-backed in the chair, seemingly impenetrable in leather and denim. She wanted more?

His imagination meandered down paths she surely wouldn't have intended. Visions of cracking through that tough veneer with his questing lips on her body. Peeling away those layers till he had her in her corset and boots. Laying her out on the bed. Fingers stroking her honeyed skin. Burying themselves in her hair...

No.

He wasn't like his father, succumbing to a beautiful face and living with the consequences.

Christo swallowed. Shut down his errant thoughts.

He'd give her something, since before the night was over she'd need to trust him—if only a little. Christo reached for his jacket again, put his hand into a front pocket and retrieved her phone. He slid it across the table towards her.

Thea picked it up, checked the screen and frowned. Her eyes were tight with concern.

'Now, call for help and try to get someone to believe I'm holding you prisoner here on your wedding night...' He nodded to the mobile clasped in her hands. 'Or tell me how you got that money.'

She hesitated a short while, then her expression changed as if she'd dismissed whatever had been troubling her. A soft, knowing smile played on her lips. She was making him wait.

It had the desired effect. Christo savoured the warm lick of anticipation curling on its seductive journey through him. He might have smiled too, but he didn't want to show her he was enjoying this far more than he should.

'My father thought paid work beneath any daughter of his. But he always expected me to dress impeccably so people wouldn't talk,' she sneered. 'He paid me an occasional allowance, which Elena banked in that account. So I wouldn't be discovered, she gave me her clothes once she'd worn them a few times. Her father was a generous man, so he never noticed her constantly needing new things.'

A clever scheme—as far as it went. 'Well, it seems you're more frugal than I imagined. Lucky me. But that still doesn't explain how you accumulated so much.'

'I've been planning from the moment I turned eighteen and received my first *"pay"* for being a compliant daughter. Five years of saving. But that was never going to be enough. So I learned the stock market, investing… Turns out I was quite successful.'

Thea sat forward, talking with her eyes and body and hands. Bristling with an uncommon fire and passion. Dangerously sparking his. This woman—his wife… He now questioned whether he should have married her, or employed her.

'Do you have any investment tips for me?' Christo took another sip of his cognac.

Thea smirked. 'I hear Atlas Shipping's doing quite well. Perhaps even better now, with an advantageous marriage between its owner and the daughter of Greece's biggest banker.'

On paper, of course, she was correct. But his father's unfortunate dealings with hers had risked more than anyone knew.

'Since I own the company, investing there would be pointless. I want to diversify.'

Of course he didn't own the company quite yet. He shared it with his father. Which was what had necessitated this impossible situation.

She sighed. Rolled her eyes. 'There's a tech start-up in the States. The talk is that they've increased the capacity for solar cell efficiency to eighty percent. It'll make a small fortune.' She looked him up and down, as if inspecting something unpleasant. 'Not that you need it.'

'Name?'

'I'll let you know tomorrow,' she said. 'Once you've agreed to a divorce and given me the contents of that envelope.'

CHAPTER THREE

THEA SMILED. CHRISTO'S face wasn't so impassive now. His head was cocked to one side, pinning her with his hard green eyes. He slowly rolled the brandy balloon in his hands and took another sip.

Christo didn't want a clever wife; he wanted a compliant wife. She'd never be that, ceding her precious freedom to a husband. A quick divorce and he could find himself another woman. One who might even *like* to be with him, or to sleep in that bed which looked big enough to have a party on.

Heat flooded to her cheeks, slid through her blood. Not that she'd ever think about parties in his bed, or what sort of parties he might have there. No way.

'Unfortunately, I require a wife. Since I have you, I don't see any point looking for another.'

She clenched her hands, the edges of her mobile phone cutting into her palms. There had to be a way out of this. Alexis would know what to do if she asked, but her texts lay unanswered.

She took a few deep breaths, trying to calm the nerves roiling in her stomach. She'd come too far to fail. Time to start negotiations to release her from this disastrous union.

Although she doubted Christo had any, Thea appealed to his better judgement. 'I don't want to be your wife. And you don't want me. I *know*. Why settle for this? You could find someone else. Someone you love.'

He lounged back on the couch, impossibly masculine with his shirt part open, showing a dark sprinkling of hair on that strong chest. A shadow of growth now adorned his jaw. She'd never looked at a man before—not unfiltered like this—and he was mesmerising. He drained his drink. As he leaned forward to place his glass on the table he licked his full bottom lip. A seductive pulse sparked deep and low in her belly.

'I've no interest in love.' His lazy, heavy-lidded gaze fixed on her. Assessing. 'So, for now, I'm keeping you.'

The folded paper with her account numbers gleamed a taunting white in his hand. Christo turned it over in his fingers, flicking it backwards and forwards. But his eyes never left her.

She slumped in her chair. There was going to be no negotiation here. She was a prisoner. Just as with her father and Demetri. A pawn in some scheme between rich, powerful men.

She clenched her teeth. 'You're a monster.'

He shrugged and smiled. It should have been friendly enough, but the way he bared his perfect white teeth looked a little…carnivorous. Still, she wouldn't waver. She wasn't scared of him—not this man.

'Yes. Though on some days I'm only human,' he said. 'You'd do well to remember that.'

She glanced over at the enormous bed again. Did he mean she could buy her freedom another way? There was a *presence* about him. Muscular, powerful, superior. Maybe some women craved that in a man. Would relish running their fingers through his spiky dark hair. Live to drown in the depths of his hazel-green eyes.

She wasn't one of them.

Christo followed her gaze and looked back at her through steepled fingers.

'Tired, Thea? It has been a long day.' His perfectly etched lips tilted at the corners. 'So let's stop toying with each other. My father's will stipulates that to inherit Atlas Shipping I must have a wife. Since you've married me, I'm not letting you go till he's dead and buried.'

Threads of fear wrapped around Thea's throat, tightening till she gasped for breath. Her heart pummelled her ribs. How old was Christo's father? This could go on for years.

She couldn't.

She wouldn't…

Christo leaned forward. 'There's no point hiding the truth from you. Not now.'

How could he sit there so calmly, as if this sort of thing happened to him every day?

Her phone fell from her hand into her lap. She curled her freed fingers into her palm, concentrating on the bite of her nails on the soft flesh. Her breathing steadied.

'How's your father's health?'

Christo smiled. 'My father's ill. Terminally so. Although his condition has stabilised of late. But I appreciate your concern.'

Thea stilled. She knew too well the pain of losing a beloved parent before their time. The emptiness that followed. No matter what was happening here, she wouldn't dance around his father's waiting grave.

'That's why he wasn't at our wedding? I wondered…' she said, though it didn't explain why his mother hadn't been there either. 'I'm sorry.'

Christo waved the words away. 'Don't be. He has time.'

A chill spread through her. The man was like a glacier. Frozen, immovable. A shudder racked her body. If he didn't care about his dying father, he'd never care about what she wanted. She clenched her fists even tighter. The sharp slice of her fingernails branded her palms, yet the trembling in her limbs wouldn't stop.

'I'm not a cruel man. Although I had some fine teachers.'

His voice was gentle. Were those words supposed to be something like reassurance? Because she knew about cruelty too. Her father and Demetri were masters. She'd lived with it all her life and she saw its hallmarks in Christo. The arrogance, the superiority. The assurance that there was no other way but his.

'If you're not cruel, we can divorce.'

Her voice sounded distant, even to her own ears. The

room folded in, its walls seeming too close. Her vision faded around the edges as her pulse sped to an inhuman speed.

Not here, not now.

She breathed through the moment until everything came back into focus.

'My father hasn't long to live. Twelve months at most. So his doctors say.' He looked down at his hands, now clasped in front of him. 'I don't have time to divorce and remarry. When he dies, I'll grant what you want.'

'Why me?'

She wanted to know why she'd been chosen as a piece in this game. Her father hadn't told her, other than giving her a list of information he required about Atlas Shipping.

'You were available.'

'And you say you're not a cruel man? If that's all it needed, no doubt there were any number of women who would have thrown themselves at your feet if you'd asked.'

'I need *you*, Thea.'

His words were rich and silky and they wound around her like treacherous ribbons, tying her to the spot. She should get up…shout, rage. But she couldn't. Her skin prickled uncomfortably. She unzipped her jacket as perspiration slicked the back of her neck.

Christo went on. 'You're clearly a businesswoman, so I don't expect you to agree to this undertaking for free. Your funds will be increased and returned.'

Freedom. At a price.

She could leave now—assuming Christo let her, and that was in some doubt—but she had little doubt that if she walked out tonight, she'd go with nothing.

The curl of fear gripped her again. She'd witnessed her mother being turned against by family and friends because of her choice to escape Tito Lambros. The man she'd never loved. Even as a child Thea had recognised her mother's deprivations. Maria had always looked so thin and starved… of everything.

She'd never forgotten her mother's words of advice. *Don't do what I did. Ensure your future above all things.*

And if she left, where would she go? Elena's father and Thea's father were friends. She'd be returned to Christo and then...

No. There was only Alexis. Surely he'd done what he'd promised? Taken his money and left Greece?

The fear that he might not have began to throttle her. Dark visions chasing her and biting at her heels.

'You're thinking too hard, Thea.'

Christo's voice dripped calm patience. He was trying to seduce her into a deal with the devil. She was trapped. Exchanging one silk-lined prison for another.

'How can I trust you?' she asked.

He relaxed in the chair, a slight smile tilting his lips. He saw victory in his sights—she was sure of it. She wanted to keep him talking so she could think.

'All that I ask is we stay married until I inherit Atlas Shipping in full.' He stood and began unbuttoning the rest of his shirt. 'I'll have our negotiations committed to a formal document. A post-nuptial agreement, so to speak.'

He shrugged the crisp cotton from his shoulders, grabbed his suit jacket, her envelope and account numbers, and then turned.

'I'll give you a few moments to think about it.'

Thea froze. All she could do was watch as he strolled into a huge walk-in wardrobe. Transfixed by his broad, powerful shoulders. The way his back muscles flexed and moved with every step.

Somewhere in the depths of the room she heard the rush of a shower. Imagined hot water running over the ridges and hollows of Christo's tanned skin, taut over muscle...

Thea shook herself, lifting the spell. She needed to speak to Alexis.

Grabbing her phone, she texted.

Bluebird

Their code if she needed help. The one word he'd never ignore.

She waited for a response. Something. Anything.

No answer came.

She clenched her fists. Concentrated on the bite of her nails into her palms as she slowed her breathing.

'Have you decided?'

That deep velvet voice rolled over her, interrupting her dark thoughts. Christo wandered into the room wearing only long black silk pyjama pants, slung low around his narrow hips, where they seemed to have found an unsettling home. She couldn't tear her eyes from his elegantly muscled torso. A sprinkling of hair on his chest arrowed down his body in a line between the ridges of his abdomen, before disappearing underneath the waistband of his pyjamas.

'What are you doing?'

Her voice came out a little too high. She took in a breath. The intoxicating scent of warm soap and clean male skin teased her senses.

Christo raised his eyebrows. His hair clung damp to his head. A few drops of water still sparkled on his shoulders. 'It's been a long and exciting day. I'm preparing for bed.'

'Put on some clothes. This…' she flapped her hand about in his direction, averting her eyes '…it's impolite.'

'Since I usually sleep naked, I consider the way I'm dressed to be the height of good manners. What's your decision?'

Out on the streets with nothing, there would be little she could do to help her half-brother, if that's what he needed. Here, she had a chance. Some resources even without her money. She would put up with anything to ensure Alexis was safe. She owed him that much.

'I agree.'

She hated the smug curl of Christo's sensual mouth as she spoke.

'There are other conditions,' he said.

Thea narrowed her eyes. Of course there were. 'And they are?'

'This must, in *every* way, appear like a real marriage.'

'How does a "real marriage" appear?'

She had no idea. Her mother had left the brutality of the marital bed when Thea was young. She had no memories of anything other than the beautiful, broken woman Maria Lambros had become.

'We're happy newlyweds. Being faithful to each other is one condition. I'm sure you can use your imagination for the rest. You talked about marrying for love before.'

He walked to the huge bed, threw back the covers and lay down in masculine splendour, patting the space next to him.

'I said I wasn't sleeping with you!'

'I assumed you meant sex,' he said. Thea flushed bright and hot. The way that word slid syrupy from his tongue sounded dark, decadent and very, very dirty. 'Which has nothing to do with sleeping.'

'No. I meant I wasn't going to share your bed. Where am I going to sleep?'

'There's plenty of room here. You can trust me.'

She looked again at that enormous piece of furniture. With him all bronzed perfection like a god, at its centre. 'I'm not—'

'So you can't trust yourself?'

He smiled. And this smile wasn't predatory or wolf-like. His face lit up with warmth in his lips, dancing eyes. It made her all tight and shivery, as if she was about to burst from her skin.

'I need my own room.'

'If you move to your own room when we're newly married we'll be exposed.'

And then it dawned on her what she had really agreed to.

She'd not been concentrating as they'd talked, and Christo had outplayed her. Still, there was a possibility of rectifying the situation…

Thea waved at the sitting room area. 'A gentleman would take the couch.'

Christo sat up and skewered her with a fierce, hot glare. 'When I married you today I assumed it would be real enough. Arranged? Yes. Unwelcome? Absolutely. But real, nonetheless. That means sleeping in my bed, with my wife. None of this arrangement means I'll be relegated to the couch. If you want it, it's yours.'

He flopped back down onto the covers, with his arms behind his head.

Infuriating man.

Thea peeled away her leather jacket. Tore off her boots. She stormed into the still humid en suite bathroom, removed her top and battled with her corset, breathing a sigh as the laces were released. She cast it into a corner, slipped on her black top again and pulled the pins from her hair. They scattered on the benchtop as she raked her hands through it to untangle the braiding. She wiped off her make-up.

All right, she'd play his little game. For now. But what was she going to wear to sleep? The maids had packed her an exotic trousseau, with a variety of the skimpy nightwear her father's latest mistress deemed she required to entertain *'a man like Christo Callas'*.

The horror of that woman taking her 'under her wing', barely older than herself… Thea shuddered.

Tonight she'd sleep in her clothes, and work out the rest in the morning.

Thea marched back into the room and settled on the couch, making a show of fluffing the cushions. She needn't have. They were soft as down. In a final act of defiance, she bashed a decorative pillow into submission under her head.

Christo chuckled. 'Sleep well, Thea.'

The lights flicked off and the room was plunged into

darkness. As Thea lay there she heard Christo shift on the bed. She imagined the crisp drag of cool sheets over his semi-naked body.

'I will,' she said sweetly as the intoxicating vision rolled through her head.

She curled onto her side. And as she sank into the plump cushions the adrenalin leached away to be replaced by leaden exhaustion.

Before she fell asleep, she muttered, 'Once I overcome my dreams of smothering you in your bed…'

CHAPTER FOUR

CHRISTO ROSE AS dawn bled pale yellow through the window of his bedroom. Thea hadn't stirred. He walked past the infernal couch she'd made her bed for the past three nights. Three *long* nights. Her resolve was commendable, but his was rapidly shredding.

When he'd struck their agreement, he hadn't really considered the implications of having her so close. Every movement she made as she slept, each muffled sigh in the darkness, and he woke. He was at risk of getting no rest so long as she stayed in the room with him. And what she wore… Her nights were spent clothed in an alluring array of silk and lace which clung to her delectable body and set his on high alert.

This morning Thea lay in luxurious blue satin, split to her thigh. As she sprawled the gown parted, to reveal long, slender legs. He craved to stroke her golden skin, to wake her with gentle caresses. To hear her breathy murmurs of surprise as he coaxed her into consciousness. In his imaginings she welcomed him with a sultry smile and open arms…

He shook his head, took a slow breath. Clenched his fists, reining in the desire to touch. Madness lay at the end of these current thoughts. Their marriage was a business relationship. Nothing more. Anyhow, Thea didn't want him. She never would.

Christo threw himself under a cold shower to douse the fever of Thea raging through his blood. The needles of icy water shocked some sense into him. Once dressed, he made his way to the terrace overlooking a glittering lap pool. He ignored the breakfast of pastry, fruit and meats adorning the table. Of greater interest was the report Raul's security

firm had prepared on Thea's movements in the months before their marriage.

He'd commissioned the work with only a fleeting pang
of guilt. Tito Lambros couldn't be trusted, and Christo had
wanted to know exactly who he was marrying before sliding a ring on Thea's finger. He'd glanced at the document
before their official engagement. Uninteresting reports of
her having coffee with her best friend, shopping, the occasional nightclub. Always overseen by bodyguards. Nothing to alert anyone to the suspicion that Thea was anything
other than the dutiful, obedient, innocent daughter her father described.

Christo yawned. He sipped his bitter black coffee and
turned to the photographs. Grainy, night-time pictures. He
hadn't studied them before the wedding, preferring to rely
on the certainty of printed words. Had he chanced a look
he'd have noticed immediately. Thea and Elena swapped
clothes. Hairstyles. In a darkened venue people wouldn't
notice the difference.

Thea was right. She hid in plain sight.

The click of heels on the tiled terrace alerted him to her
approach. He slid the report into his briefcase and threw
back the dregs of his coffee. She sauntered to the table in
low-slung jeans and a heavy studded belt. A sheer, jewel-
coloured top flowed around her torso. She presented the
same contradiction now as on their wedding night: a picture of toughness softened by feminine grace.

For a startling moment he craved to strip her down and
discover where the toughness ended and the woman began.

'Good morning,' she said, and sat.

Reaching for a fig, she tore the ruby flesh in half. Her
lips wrapped around the luscious fruit as she took a bite.
Watching her sleep was an ordeal for even the most pious
man, but witnessing her eat was a study in erotic torture.
He adjusted himself in his seat. Thanked all things holy that

he could remain at the table for as long as it took to wrestle the pounding hammer of need into submission.

As Thea consumed the mouthful of fig she rubbed her neck, oblivious to his crushing desire to kiss the juice of that fruit from her lips till she moaned his name. He cleared his throat. Quelled the fantasy. She'd probably bite him, not kiss back.

'Poor sleep?'

'I'm sore from the couch.'

'You should've asked me for proper pillows.'

'I want my own room. There's no privacy. No way to keep the mystery alive between us.'

Thea fluttered her long lashes. The glorious flirtation of her... Was this how his father had been trapped all those years ago? At least Raul's report gave no indication that Thea had a lover stashed in some safe corner, ready to resume their relationship at a moment's notice, like his mother had. Sad how he counted that as a blessing rather than an expectation.

Christo poured another thick, dark coffee and leaned back in his chair. 'We're newlyweds. Tangling the bed sheets with passion every night. We don't want there to be any mystery.'

The carnal visions rioting through his head made him wish his words were true, rather than a pretence.

Anna came to the table. She bustled about arranging food, collecting plates. Thea's lips tilted in a wicked smile as she stabbed a piece of meat with her fork. He had little doubt she wanted it to be his flesh under those sharp tines.

'But, Christo, *darling*. I look haggard. Of course I need my own room,' she said, with the perfect pitch of complaint. 'Anna, come here. You'll agree. Don't I look exhausted?'

Anna sidled over to them, panic written all over her face. What was Thea up to?

'See—I look too horrid for Anna even to answer.'

The girl tried to run off, but Thea clamped a hand on her arm, pinning her to the spot.

'No, stay. I'm not getting any sleep.'

Christo took another sip from his cup, schooling his face to one of polite interest. 'There are good reasons for that. Which no one needs to hear…'

He understood now. He'd been witness to all his mother's games over the years. This was no different.

'Anna does.' Thea looked at Anna, brows drawn, face serious. 'He snores. Terribly. All night.'

The coffee caught in his throat. He lurched forward. Coughed.

'I don't!'

Thea's wide-eyed innocence continued. 'He doesn't want to admit it… I'm sure he's quite embarrassed.'

Nowhere in their bargain was there any term allowing her to make a fool of him in front of his staff. His voice was a low growl of warning. *'Thea…'*

She ignored him, focusing on Anna, whose look of horror might have been comical in other circumstances. 'Now I'm getting dark rings under my eyes. Soon I'll stop looking beautiful and Christo won't want me anymore.'

'I'll buy you some earplugs.'

Thea lowered her voice to a conspiratorial whisper. 'That won't work. He's a beast, I tell you. Why, last night—'

His chair scraped in protest along the tiles as he stood. Jaw clenched tight. Breathing hard.

'Enough.' The lies and manipulation stopped now. 'Let Anna go before you horrify her any further.'

Thea released her grip and Anna ran back into the house. He sat. Took a drink of water. Attempted to cool the anger boiling his blood.

'What is it about the words "real marriage" that you don't understand?'

'The pronouncement that I had to share your room came after I'd agreed to this arrangement of ours.' She crossed her arms, eyes narrowing. 'That was underhanded. And as far as I'm concerned it doesn't form part of our original agreement.'

He threw up his hands. 'You're trying to win this argument on a *technicality*?'

'No. I'd prefer to talk about what the marriages I know of are actually like. My parents didn't share a room. What about yours?'

His parents weren't an example of marriage to which he aspired. Not that marriage was a state he'd ever thought he'd find himself in until that final argument with his father. But he didn't want to give her any more ammunition.

He stretched his neck from side to side. It gave an audible and satisfying crack.

'My parents weren't traditional in many things.'

Their relationship had been one of mutually assured destruction. His father had loved his mother. His mother had loved the Callas fortune. A pregnancy and Christo's birth had secured her future in a neat package.

'So why do we need to be?' Thea flicked her hair over her shoulders and pouted.

For all her theatrics, her lips were pink and dangerously kissable.

'If you loved me, you'd let me have my own room.'

He'd learned from childhood that love and marriage were lies. And a caring family the biggest lie of them all.

Christo dropped his voice to a whisper. 'Since I don't love you, what you say is meaningless.'

'That's the problem.'

Thea leaned forward, her hands splayed on the table. Christo's gaze dropped as the front of her sheer top fell open.

'If you were pretending to love me properly it's what you'd do.'

Was she guileless enough not to know that her position allowed him a perfect view of her magnificent cleavage?

All silky skin and powerful temptation? Probably not. He suspected Thea didn't do anything without good reason and a great deal of thought.

He stared for a moment longer than he ought, then pinched the bridge of his nose. 'You're a manipulator.'

'You're heartless.'

Thea flopped back into her seat, hands clenched tight on the damask tablecloth. Her colour faded till she was as pale as the white fabric under her hands. Something about it twisted tight in his gut.

Since when had he started developing a conscience? This was a business deal like any other. Though how he was going to survive another night, let alone another year with her in his room was anyone's guess.

Then, over Thea's shoulder, he spied movement. He reached out to take her clenched hand in his. Her eyes widened and she tried to tug away.

'We're being watched by my staff,' he said, and she stilled. He pasted what he hoped was a warm smile on his face. 'Whilst they're paid well to be discreet, I'd prefer to give them nothing to talk about.'

Christo rubbed his thumb over Thea's knuckles, trying to appear affectionate and attentive. Her eyes dropped to where he stroked gently back and forth, and the barest flush tinted her cheeks. Such a beautiful colour on her golden skin. A glow kindled deep inside him.

'All I was trying to say is that a man would do anything for the woman he truly loves.' Her voice was a whisper, gentle as the breeze through the olive tree above them.

'Where did you hear that?'

Thea's hand relaxed, smooth and warm in his. Her skin was a marvel of liquid silk under his fingers. So soft… How would the rest of her feel?

'Someone told me once,' she said, 'when counselling me to demand more from life.'

Those words pulled him back from his silent imaginings.

He'd never had to compromise for anyone. Although what Thea said had a ring of truth to it. They were supposed to be an adoring couple. Their love would have the power to make them do irrational things. Like lifting her hand to his lips. Anna was still watching, after all. Anyhow, it was only a light touch over her perfect skin. Yet he couldn't stop.

'Wh-what are you doing?'

He closed his eyes for a moment. Savoured her exotic scent of honey and spice. 'Pretending to love you properly,' he murmured.

What if they made the physical aspects of this marriage real, for as long as they had each other? It would be some sort of solution to what promised to become a long stretch of sleepless nights.

Thea's lips parted, all of her soft and languid. Her pupils were huge and dark. He could lean across the table and kiss her now. Start a seduction so complete the word *no* would leave her vocabulary for ever.

But his father's words echoed in his mind. *'I know you, son. Marry, and nature will take care of the rest.'*

A chill ran through him. He was not that man.

He released her. Pulled away. Suffered the cold loss of her hand in his.

'Ask me,' Christo said.

Hector didn't know him at all. He was stronger than his father and he'd prove it.

'For what?'

Her voice was low and husky, scraping across his skin as surely as her fingernails would. So affecting he could almost feel the erotic sting. He craved it. Ignored it.

'Your own room. No lies. No manipulation.'

She opened her mouth. Hesitated for a moment, as if asking for anything was foreign to her. 'Christo, I'd like my own room.'

'See? That wasn't difficult.'

'You haven't given me an answer yet.' A faint frown

marred her brow. 'What about this needing to appear like a real marriage?'

'That requirement hasn't changed.' He knew of one solution, but part of him wanted her to give something herself. Then he'd consider it a small victory. 'What can you offer me in return?'

Another flush of pink coloured her cheeks as Thea reached up to toy with the pendant hanging from a fine gold chain around her neck. 'If I have my own room, I could come to yours for a little while each night, so your people won't ask questions.'

And there it was. Not ideal, but he supposed compromise never was. At least he might get some unbroken sleep without Thea's glorious temptation sprawled out before him each night, burning his blood.

'You'll stay for a *long* while,' he said, sipping at his now cool coffee. 'I'm supposed to be making insatiable love to a beautiful woman. That's something I like to take my time with.'

She licked her lips. It hit him like a kick in the groin.

'What will we really be doing?' she asked.

He shrugged as Anna began another nervous approach to the table. 'For all I care you can do a crossword.'

When Anna reached them, she gave a discreet cough. 'Mr Callas, your mechanic's here.'

'Thank you. And, Anna? Mrs Callas and I have discussed her request. Please make up the spare room next to mine and move all her things in there. Today.'

He looked over at Thea, softened his gaze. Tried to muster an enamoured expression. He wasn't sure whether it worked, so his words would have to suffice. 'I'd do anything to ensure my bride's happiness here.'

Thea flashed a smile in response, relieved and yet dazzling. It curled into him, flickered into life a beguiling warmth in his chest. Odd how this new agreement between them felt so enjoyable...

He stood, before the sensation ran away with him completely.

'Tonight, *koukla mou*,' he said, kissing her on the cheek, relishing her soft exhalation as he did.

And as he walked away he found himself counting the moments till he saw her again.

CHAPTER FIVE

THEA SAT ON the edge of her new bed, in her new room, hands tightly clenched. Concentrating on the cut of her fingernails into her palms.

Pretending to love. Pretending.

Her whole life was a pretence. Faking her role as a dutiful daughter, a happy bride.

The pain of it knotted inside her, tighter and tighter. She breathed slowly through the gnawing in her stomach. And yet for a fleeting moment she'd snatched a glimpse of another life. The touch of a man. Her *husband*. The soft press of his lips on her hand. The burn it had left. How, for a breathtaking second, she'd craved something more and her heart had filled with silly, jagged if-onlys which had cut on every beat.

But this was more pretence. Marriage formed no part of her plans. Even in her short life she'd seen enough. Knew that husbands ruled, and heaven help any woman caught by circumstance or, even worse, love. She'd never succumb to it. It was a romantic trap set for the foolhardy. That was when the bars truly fell, clanging into place for ever.

She shivered, wrapping her arms round her waist. She had her plan. What she needed was to find Alexis. To ease the constant ache of fear in her chest. To prove her agreement with Christo was good for something.

Time for the next charade.

She stood, smoothing her palms over her clothes, relieved that at least she didn't have to deal with the teasing caress of silken lingerie sliding over her body. Or the hot gleam from Christo's eyes which had taunted her for the past three nights.

That man pretended too. His appearance of a tightly

reined-in gentleman was an act. She'd seen the way he'd looked at her as she'd lain on the couch in his room. As if she was a meal set out for his pleasure. All that dark hunger had tempted Thea to spread herself out and be devoured.

But it would never happen. He'd used her for his own ends and she'd take what she could from him, no questions.

Having her own room was a win, and in her life she'd had too few. It wasn't as big as Christo's, and was all soft neutrals—a blank, pale canvas like her life so far.

Thea dreaded leaving its silence and safety, but she padded down the hall with book and pencil in hand, her toes sinking into the velvety carpet. The doors to his suite were closed when she arrived. She raised her hand and knocked.

'Come.'

His deep, low voice slid over her like a rush of warm water. Thea hesitated, then took a steadying breath and entered the room.

Christo sat on the couch in jeans and a T-shirt, the clothes soft and well worn. His shirt looked bound to the sculpted muscles of his chest and biceps. The jeans outlined his powerful thighs. Her stomach flipped with a curious disappointment. But no, she definitely *didn't* miss the expanse of bronzed skin and naked torso he'd subjected her to as he'd slept on his huge bed.

Out of suit trousers and bespoke shirts he looked young. Thea supposed he was—though at thirty-one Christo was hardly Greece's youngest billionaire. And, unlike his usual stern poise during the day when his employees were present, tonight there was something almost approachable about him, with his hair raked through and messy, a few strands falling across his brow.

The observation tugged low and warm in her belly, pooling in a way that made her shift on the spot. But it was something on which she refused to dwell. Instead, she did a prancing little twirl.

'I wasn't sure how to dress.' She waved her hands between them as she looked down at her black leggings and oversized grey top. 'For this...assignation.'

His eyes met hers, then took a meandering journey over her silhouette. Even though her body was hidden under formless clothes it was as if he could see right through them.

'What you wear is immaterial, since the aim of newly-weds is to get out of their clothes as quickly as possible.'

All she envisaged was searching hands and naked limbs entwined. Breathless sighs and a deep, unrelenting ache.

She shut out the errant thoughts and flopped into the overstuffed armchair opposite. 'Charming.'

The corners of his mouth tilted in a lazy smile. 'If you pretended to be more of an adoring wife, I'd show you how charming I could be.'

She ignored the invitation. 'I'm here, aren't I?'

'You could try to look happy about it.'

She tossed her head, meaning to look resolute, but the move seemed somehow childish.

'Never.'

'Never is a long, cold time to be alone.' He ran his thumb over the full curve of his lower lip.

Such a decadent mouth for a man...

'I'm used to being alone,' she said.

Christo's eyes tightened for a heartbeat, almost in a wince, then it was gone.

'So am I.'

She dismissed him with a bored, practised glance and tucked her feet under her, opening the book Anna had purchased for her that afternoon. The request had earned her a bemused look, but she'd assured Anna that Christo loved doing puzzles in his spare time. When Anna had cackled out loud at this revelation, she knew she'd found a friend in the house.

Thea grinned.

One down. Six letters.

The tallest mountain in Europe.

She scribbled the answer.

'Crosswords?' Christo chuckled, deep and low.

The sound rolled over her, making her thighs clench.

She shrugged. 'Your suggestion.'

He tossed down the papers he'd been studying. 'I'm flattered you listened. So you're planning on becoming an obedient wife? Lucky me.'

'I wouldn't get my hopes up if I were you.'

'Ah, so my luck's running out already?' he said, sprawling on the couch.

Thea nibbled the end of her pencil and a dark and slumberous look swept over Christo's face. She ignored the awareness of it prickling at the base of her spine.

'Now hope is all I have left,' he added.

'Whilst you're hoping for something which won't happen, you can help. Two across. Eight letters. *"A large Patagonian rodent that lives in communal groups."*'

He stretched back, hands behind his head. His shirt shifted to expose a glorious slice of golden etched abdomen.

'Capybara.'

She pencilled in the word, which fitted. 'How do you know that?'

'I've tasted it.'

'What?' she squeaked. 'But a rodent's a rat.'

'More like a guinea pig. No tail.'

'Well, having no tail obviously makes *all* the difference.'

'Not my fondest culinary memory, but I was in South America on business and politeness dictated I sample it.'

Christo smiled. A wicked, glinting thing.

'I didn't realise I'd find crosswords so enjoyable. What's our next clue?'

He was teasing her. It lit up his face with a mischievous sort of amusement. She tried hard not to smile herself. She shouldn't be having fun. She shouldn't. Reality would intrude soon enough.

Thea shut the crossword book. 'I don't want to risk hearing about any more of your odd culinary extravaganzas.'

'Not my experience with sea cucumbers in China? Where's your sense of adventure?'

'I've never been encouraged to have one.'

'Shame... I'm travelling to New York in a few weeks. I thought you might join me.'

Her heart leapt. He was going to the city her mother had promised to take her.

An awful yearning replaced the sense of fun. It clutched at her, twisting hard. She toyed with the corner of the book in her lap, staring out past filmy curtains to the floodlit balcony. The illuminated olive trees waved silvery in the night breeze.

'I've never been out of Greece.'

Christo leaned forward, forearms on his thighs. His wedding ring glinted in the lights. 'What was your father thinking?'

That if he kept her in a cage she wouldn't fall, like her mother had before her marriage.

'He's protective. There was always a driver. Always a bodyguard. Something I rely on now.'

The lie caught in her throat. Her father had been her jailer. Demetri his enforcer.

'Come to New York with me and you'll have a driver. I'll also organise one of my security detail to attend you. If that's what you want.'

It was. Desperately. Because here was her way to locate Alexis. Christo had power and reach she didn't. If anyone could find him it was her husband.

'I'd like to bring my own bodyguard.'

'My men are all provided by Raul. Highly trained and supremely trustworthy.'

Could she tell him the truth about Alexis? That he was

the child her mother had been forced to relinquish? Her half-brother, who'd kept her going on her darkest days?

No lies. No manipulation.

No. She couldn't trust anyone who did business with her father—especially if that business involved her.

She licked her lips. 'I only trust Alexis Anastos—the man my father engaged.'

Christo lounged in his chair, but there was a tension about him which told her he was watchful.

'Where is he now?'

'I'm not sure. He was released prior to our marriage. Said he was going to take a long holiday. Something about working with me making him need one.' She laughed. It sounded hollow.

Christo's eyes narrowed. His body stilled with predator-like intent.

'How close were you to him?'

The question was measured, quiet. But the implication of the words burrowed under her skin. What did he think she was? A hot roil of anger seethed inside her. Newly married and already seeking out someone else? Anyhow, they had an agreement—one she loathed, but she'd stick by it nonetheless.

'He was like the brother I should have had!' she snapped.

Christo cocked his head. *Stupid.* Her emotion would give everything away.

Thea levelled him with a steady gaze. 'Besides, I'm not his type.'

That seemed to relax the crouching panther a little.

Christo settled back into the comfortable cushions of the couch. 'Let me know the security firm he works for and I'll look into it.'

She breathed out slowly. 'Thank you.'

'I said I'd do anything to make you happy here.'

That voice. Soft as the caress of silk sheets. But his eyes held the promise of a brewing storm. And she wasn't even sure he was trying. If he did, Thea knew the man would beat the devil in his ability to tempt.

'Are you really going to insist on doing this every evening?'

'I seem to recall you offered.'

'It was the lesser of two evils.'

'A similar position for both of us,' Christo said. 'We could try to get to know each other, since we might be together some time.'

Thea's stomach churned like a twisting pit of vipers. This could go on for years. Yet she couldn't pray for his father's death to free her any faster.

Her pulse leapt, threatening to rampage out of control. Her breathing became short and shallow. These episodes had increased in their relentless frequency since her engagement. An old, bitter enemy challenging her from the shadows. But she wouldn't let it consume her in front of Christo.

Thea flipped the pencil in her hand and pressed the sharp point into the pad of her thumb, concentrating on the pain. Her heartbeat slowed. The twist in her stomach eased. She relaxed the pencil's pressure and rubbed the spot with her index finger, soothing the sting.

'So, what? We play twenty questions?'

He smiled in that wolfish way of his and her toes curled into the plush carpet.

'Would you prefer truth or dare?' he asked.

'I'm a bit old for that sort of game.' She sniffed. In reality, she'd never played *any* sort. Though she'd always craved the freedom to make mistakes of her own.

'What would you like to play?' Christo asked, his tone all soft invitation.

Could he have been one of those mistakes, if she'd been allowed to make them? In other circumstances might she have fallen for the ruinous gleam in those gold-green eyes or the dark promise in his midnight voice?

No. He wasn't her mistake to make. Now or ever.

She sighed. Rolled her eyes for added effect. 'Ask your questions, Christo.'

Christo stood and walked to the bureau, where he poured himself a cognac. He sipped the drink as he regarded her over the rim of the glass. 'My mechanic was impressed with your bike. Where did you develop an interest in vintage British motorcycles?'

Her heart stopped for a beat. In truth, before becoming *her* interest it had been Alexis's passion. She had to step carefully. Christo didn't really want to get to know her. He was littering their conversation with landmines to trap her.

'And here I thought you were going to ask me my favourite colour. Which, for the record, is red.'

'Why does that not surprise me?' he said, smiling. 'Mine's green.'

'Opposites.'

'They can attract.'

'I'm thinking oil and water.'

'And I'm thinking you're avoiding my question.'

Clever man.

She tried for her most guileless look. 'I like the glossy black paint and glistening chrome.'

Which was what she saw the day Alexis had proudly delivered her gift—a classic of British motorcycling. Then he'd taught her to ride. Hours with the wind in her face, as if she was flying. And she'd finally understood the glory of the machine and the joy of freedom.

'You don't strike me as the sort of woman who'd make a decision because something looks shiny.'

The corners of Christo's appraising eyes crinkled in amusement, softening the inherent hardness of him.

'Sorry to disappoint.'

Christo raised his glass to her with a slow smile. She couldn't take her eyes from his perfect lips, the sensual way they curved. A slick of warmth bloomed deep inside her, aching to be satisfied in a way she'd never allow.

'I find you intriguing. Plenty of time for disappointment later.'

Her breathing hitched. He wasn't supposed to find anything about her interesting. 'Aren't I supposed to be asking some questions too?'

'I'm not finished with you yet.'

Christo strolled back to his seat and sprawled on the couch in apparent indolence. She knew better. He watched her like a predator stalking from the shadows.

'I don't think this is how the game is supposed to be played,' she said.

'My rules.'

'It's unfair. And I'd never marry a man who was.'

He placed his hand over his heart. 'You wound me. As your husband, I can't have you thinking that. Ask your question.'

'Why did your father force you to marry?'

There was that tightness round his eyes again. Christo tossed back his drink. She watched the fascinating bob of his Adam's apple as he swallowed.

'Because I intended to enjoy a bachelor's life for ever. No marriage. No children.'

Children?

Thea tried to relax, resting her hands carefully in her lap. If only she could stop them trembling.

'Is there something you haven't told me? Your father didn't demand a child in the terms of his will?'

A dark, brooding shadow passed across his face. He wasn't looking at her, concentrating instead on the shimmering tumbler in his hand. It was her first sense that he had secrets himself.

The silence stretched. And then, 'No. Hector's uncouth, but that would be vulgar even for him. And I would have told you about the requirement if he had. Though who knows what he'd demand if he suspected this marriage is a sham?'

'When are we going to meet your father, to prove it's everything he hoped for?'

His eyes snapped to hers. That focus was relentless. She didn't look away. She'd never been cowed by a man before, no matter how many times her father had tried. She wasn't starting tonight.

Christo leaned forward with cautious deliberation, placing his glass on the table in front of him. 'You'll meet him when you've learned to play the role of wife to my satisfaction.'

'I'm doing an excellent job as your wife.'

'This morning?' His eyes narrowed. 'That fiction about my snoring like a hibernating bear?'

'Don't be dramatic.'

'You called me a *beast*.' A tiny muscle at his temple gave a satisfying twitch. 'Then at dinner you told Anna I had an obsession with ear and nose hair growth.'

'I was trying to be friendly. Women always complain about their husbands.'

It was another thing she and Anna laughed about. It had been such a long time since she'd laughed about anything.

'Anyhow, I read somewhere it's something men think about. Often.'

'Perhaps you need a lesson in what men think about.'

The low growl of warning made her shiver in anticipation. She glanced at the huge bed. The soft pillows. Crisp white sheets.

Thea turned back to him. 'There's *nothing* I want to learn from you.'

'Are you sure?' he asked softly. 'If you change your mind, all you have to do is ask. Nicely.'

'Your vain hope's begun to delude you. My presence is obviously a bad influence.'

That tight band in her chest gripped her again. Pressing harder. She needed to get out of here. To breathe something more than the scent of him, which curled through her with every inhalation and lit fires inside.

'May I go now?'

He shrugged. 'If you want.'

She stood. He watched, as if he'd assessed her and found her wanting. Like her father. But she could do this. If he found Alexis, everything would be worth it. She grabbed her book and made for the door.

'*Thea.*'

The cold command in his voice stopped her.

'No woman I'm sleeping with leaves my room looking like you do.'

A superior smile played on his lips. She wanted to wipe it from his face.

'And how's that?'

'So completely untouched.'

Was this simply a terrible game to entertain a bored rich man? Her blood pumped hard and hot. She tossed her book and pen on a table. Tipped her head upside down and scratched her fingers through her hair till it was a tangled mess. Wiped her palm roughly across her lips so the gloss smeared.

'There. Better?' she sneered, hands on hips. 'Or should I tear my clothes as well?'

His lips narrowed a fraction in displeasure. Excellent. Some hint that she'd affected him.

Thea whipped round to leave. She didn't hear the silent footsteps marking his approach. Only sensed his heat as he moved close. She turned, her back against the cool wood of the door, tipping her head up to look at him. She was trapped by his devilish lips, the slash of high cheekbones. And his eyes... Sparkling and shimmering, like water in sunlight. Angry. Arresting.

She couldn't move. His perfect fingers teased along her jaw, slipping down her throat and behind her head. An exquisite burn was left by his touch. She knew he could snap her. Break her like a twig. But the languid softness in his eyes said nothing of anger or hurting.

Another hand settled on her waist. Hot. Possessive. The atmosphere took on a life of its own. Trembling with the spark between them. His thumb traced the line of her lower lip. A whisper of a caress. Setting her body alight. The world blurred and her lips parted as if there would never be enough air to breathe.

He drew her close and she pressed into him. Hands on his chest. Liquid heat between her thighs. She should push him away, but those muscles under her palms... Sculpted. Like stone. Every morsel of him was too male, too much.

His mouth dropped to hers and her mind blanked. She breathed the scent of him, cool and crisp like the mountains, full of wild thyme and rosemary and pine. His lips coaxed. Encouraged. Probed. Too gentle for this man. She fought not to succumb, but his hold on her and his wicked mouth dragged her under. She'd give everything for the feel of his tongue as it explored and danced with hers.

His hand was in her hair, the hardness contrasting with his gentle lips. And the seduction of it drizzled over her like honey. Drowning her in its sticky sweetness. The dark, luscious kiss deepened and took her into the abyss. Her control shredded, ripped away as her body thrummed with primal need.

She wrapped her arms around his neck. Pulled him down. If she was to drown, he'd drown right with her. And as she fell into the intoxicating rhythm of their breaths and lips and tongues he pulled back.

She gasped. Christo turned her, his arms banding her waist. Holding her upright because she'd fall if he didn't. His lips at her ear. And she looked in the mirror opposite, saw herself. A wanton creature she didn't recognise. With wild hair and passion-drugged eyes. Red moist lips and her chest heaving. Her nipples tight and proud against the soft knit fabric of her top.

'That—' he pointed to the mirror '—is what a woman who leaves my room looks like.'

He let her go and she stumbled. The heat of him, gone. Everything, cold. He looked at her with a face which told her nothing. No sign of the kiss that had almost destroyed her marred his perfect features.

'Now you're ready to see my father.'

CHAPTER SIX

THE OLD MAN was hunched in a wheelchair in the oppressive wood-panelled library, a blanket round his legs, living the wheezing, broken half-life left to him by his dying heart. Though none of that stopped his rheumy eyes scrutinising Thea with an intensity belying his age and ill health.

Christo leaned against a dark-stained bookcase. She was executing her role as new bride to perfection. Hector would never guess their arrangement, so superb was her performance.

She was pandering to his father. And every glorious, gracious smile was driving Christo to hell.

He'd sworn never to succumb to Hector's weakness for a beautiful woman, only to find himself trapped by a viper cleverly disguised. Yet here he was, teetering on the brink. And all because of a kiss which had been meant to challenge Thea's claim that there was nothing he could teach her.

Vanity—that was what it had been about. The moment their lips had touched, when she'd responded as if he was everything she'd always craved, reason had escaped him. And now he couldn't think of anything but the drugging wonder of her plush mouth. Of immersing himself in her body till he drowned. Never coming up for air.

Her throaty, musical laugh dragged him to other thoughts. To the memory of her curves in his arms. To the smell of sweet spice and a warmth that had curled inside and licked at the cold heart of him.

He'd left the flame kindling for a while. Soaked in that tempting heat before extinguishing it. There were things about Thea he mustn't forget. His investigations into her former bodyguard, Alexis, proved she was a woman held together by lies. Cleverly woven, but lies nonetheless.

He knew all about lies. About a war of attrition being fought through a child.

'If your mother comes for your birthday, I'll buy you a puppy.'

As if he'd ever had any control over what his mother did. But he'd asked, and begged. Like any little boy wanting something badly enough. Extracting promises that had always been broken. His mother had never come. He'd never owned a dog. He'd been raised on lies, like tainted sugar stirred into his milk.

Christo clenched his teeth against the burn of acid in his gut.

'We should leave, Hector. You seem tired.' He motioned to a nurse hovering nearby.

'When I'm dead I'll have all the rest I need.'

His father didn't look at him. Only at Thea, sitting opposite. Ignoring Christo like he always did.

What irritated him more than discovering Thea's untruths was her obvious belief that he wouldn't find out. Did she think him a fool?

She laughed at something Hector said and his father gazed back, mesmerised. Yes, she did. Thea believed she could con them all.

Soon enough he'd show her how easy she'd been to expose.

'You're kind to an old man,' Hector said, patting her hand, which sat on his knee. 'A rare and precious beauty.'

She shone like an angel, perfect in a cream sheath dress that skimmed her curves and highlighted her honeyed skin.

'Not too old to pretend to charm,' Christo muttered.

Hector peered up at him, dusky lips stretched in a thin, disapproving line. A look so familiar it was etched for ever in Christo's brain. *This* was the father he knew—the one who had constantly reminded him he was a mistake. A child that no one wanted. A child who should never have been born.

'I speak the truth. She is beautiful like Maria.'

Christo pushed away from the bookcase. This can of worms shouldn't be opened. Not here. Not now. He suppressed a snarl. He'd never let Thea know the extent of his indebtedness to her father, because that would give her a power over him he couldn't allow. He *wouldn't* lose Atlas to his father's foolishness.

His eyes narrowed in warning, but Hector focused his attention on Thea.

'You knew my mother?' she asked. She toyed with a thin chain clasped at her throat, the hunger for any morsel of information written in wide-eyed desperation on her face.

'We all knew each other back then.' His father smiled wistfully.

That could be the reason why Hector had sought loans from the Lambros bank, believing an old acquaintance wouldn't foreclose on him. More poor judgement that Christo could not forgive.

'She was a bird of paradise. Your father wanted to cage her. He never could. So she flew away.'

'You think I'm like her?'

'Yes. Does my son try to cage you?'

The old man was no fool. He must have some inkling as to why Christo had chosen Thea as his bride.

Christo's stomach clenched as Thea turned to look into the soul of him with mournful, over-bright eyes.

'Why would you say that about your own son?' she asked, sounding incredulous, though the slight tremor in her voice betrayed her. 'He's taking me to New York.'

'Such pretty lies. You're a clever girl. I knew you'd make him a good wife.'

Bile rose sour in Christo's throat. The gall of it. This from the man who'd invited an enemy to slip craven fingers into his birthright. Into the company he'd earned with his own blood. Through each abandonment by his mother. Every rejection by his father. The debts Hector had incurred would take a lifetime to undo—if that Gordian knot could even be unravelled.

Christo had done his duty. This farce had gone on long enough. He strolled towards Thea. Touched her gently on the shoulder and ignored her tremble under his hand.

'*Koukla mou.* Our flight's this evening. We should leave.'

'You must come again,' Hector said, to Thea alone. 'This old man doesn't have enough company.'

She squeezed the parchment-thin skin of his father's arm. Did she see through the cruel glint in Hector's eye? Perhaps. But her voice was all sparkle and flirtation.

'How can I resist? Your son's overworked. Whenever you feel lonely, please call. No doubt I'll be feeling lonely too.'

Her words tugged at parts of him long dead. Threatening to rouse them from the grave where they'd been safely buried. Lonely was being shunted off to other people to be cared for on school breaks. Lonely was having only servants to talk to for days. Lonely was recognising the one truth in your life. That your parents didn't want you.

His father beckoned for the nurse. As she came to take the old man away he looked at Christo, his eyes filled with a wicked fire. He waggled his finger and cackled as the nurse wheeled him down the hall.

'Don't leave this one alone for too long, son, or she might run away too.'

Christo settled into the comfort of his limousine, the blood freezing through his veins. His father always did that to him—left him colder than the Arctic.

He looked at Thea and the chill thawed with a sliding heat. Her gaze dropped to his lips and a flush of colour swept over her cheeks. The throb of hunger started low in his gut.

Against his better judgement she intoxicated him. One moment all flash and fire, the next moment beautiful blushes. He could lean across the seat, right here, in this warm car filled with her scent of honey and spice. Slide a hand behind her neck and kiss her till she melted with wanting him. Call her out as the liar he knew her to be.

Which was all the reminder he needed to pull back from these delusions.

'You played your part well. There's no need to subject yourself to my father again.'

She cocked her head. 'Why do you hate him?'

Christo undid the buttons on his shirt cuffs. Rolled the sleeves up. Thirty-one years of parental contempt layered tarry and thick. Nothing could wash *that* stain away. And then, when it had come time to take what was his—when what he'd been born to do had been so close he could have caressed it with the tips of his fingers—Hector had almost thrown it away. He didn't care about Christo at all.

'Fathers and their sons.' He shrugged. These were weaknesses he'd never disclose, because weaknesses could be exploited. 'That's the way it's been even before Zeus and Cronus.'

Thea stared out through the window, absentmindedly scratching at her knee. 'Not in my experience. My brother and father are close. Partners in every crime.'

He stiffened. How much did she know about her father's and brother's activities? He suspected she despised both men. In that way, their views on their fathers were strikingly similar. The rest he could only imagine. Tito and Demetri were too careful. Even Raul had come up with nothing.

What would Thea share if she was asked the right way?

He watched her white-tipped nails digging into the flesh above the hem of her dress. Pricks of red bloomed under her skin.

'Are you all right?'

He leaned over and placed his hand on hers. Thea's slender fingers were cool and tempting under his. He drifted his thumb over the back of her hand. She turned to him, eyelids heavy and slumberous, her raspberry lips parted as if it were hard to breathe.

He looked back to where he touched her. Glorying at her silky skin, paler than his. Light to his dark. So tempting to slide higher. To stroke his errant fingers along the flesh of her inner thigh and watch those golden eyes glaze with need. See if she'd gasp and yield, relax her legs and allow him to explore all her honeyed dark places till she sighed his name and clenched around his fingers as she came.

He could do that in the back of this quiet car, with no sound bar her shallow breaths and the low thrum of the engine. Trapped in this tiny world of their own.

Time slowed, the moment pregnant with anticipation as his pulse pounded with desire. Did she feel it too?

As he looked up at her Thea's eyes widened, her gaze flicked away and she jerked her hand from under his as if burned.

No, clearly not.

Christo sat back in his seat once more, ignoring the roar of blood coursing in his ears.

'Something bit me.' Thea smoothed the hem of her dress over the red mark on her thigh and clasped her hands in her lap, fingers twisting. 'Anna says when we get to New York we're staying in your apartment near Central Park. She seems excited.'

Christo accepted the brisk change of subject. It was safer this way, when all he craved was to touch. To push. His body didn't listen to sense when he was around her. It *wanted*—like a fractious child grasping for a jar of sweets placed out of reach. And Thea was the last woman he should desire. He'd discovered things about her. Secrets and lies.

The time would soon be arriving to show her he was no fool. He'd never be fooled again.

'I've a gift to keep you company whilst we're away,' he said.

Now to see how well she'd handle what he'd found out, and how fine an actress she was.

'Ooh, goody.' She rubbed her hands together with mock glee. 'What is it? A puppy?'

Christo stilled. Ignored the pang in his chest. No. Assuming his specifications had been met, his gift wasn't something she'd be able to tame and train.

'I'm not sure you're mature enough for that responsibility,' he said as the car slid through his home's open gates and pulled into the garage.

He led her to his study. A quiet, book-lined room where fortunes had been made and lost. Nothing had been lost since he'd acquired the house. Thea was to thank for that, but she'd never know it.

He sank into the chair behind his huge desk.

'I can hardly bear the thrill of it all,' she said.

Yet she hovered in the corner of the room. Tense, as if she was a woman who hated surprises.

There was a rap at the door.

'Come.'

In walked a hulk of a man. Christo recognised him. He was one of Raul's operatives, who'd been assigned for a month to go over the house's security before he and Thea married. He was perfect. Taciturn. Incorruptible. Raul had chosen well. Thea wouldn't wrap *this* man around her little finger, as she'd obviously done to so many others.

'Thea, meet Sergei Ivanov.'

A deep frown marred her forehead as she looked Sergei up and down. 'Who the hell is he?'

Christo leaned back in the leather of his chair and smiled. 'Your new bodyguard.'

She stiffened. 'I don't want him. I want Alexis.'

Now the game began.

Christo moved from behind his desk to lean against its front corner. He'd investigated her former bodyguard out of curiosity, though he'd never have employed a man who'd missed so much. It meant Alexis was either careless or complicit. From what he'd learned, complicit seemed more likely. Although there was more to it than that…

'Sergei comes highly credentialed, with impeccable qualifications for the role.'

Thea wouldn't look at him, her eyes darting instead to Sergei's massive form. 'Impeccable qualifications for a jailer. Were they your instructions?'

'You said you'd become reliant on a bodyguard.' Christo folded his arms. 'Sergei's brief is to keep you safe.'

'I won't feel safe with him.' Her hand reflexively slid the small coin-sized pendant backwards and forwards along the chain round her neck. 'I want—'

'Alexis. I know.'

She was a clever woman—she had to see he'd caught her out. But Thea stood there, tall and defiant. He'd give her a chance to redeem herself, to tell the truth once and for all.

'I'm wondering why you want him so badly. Is there anything I need to know?'

She licked her lips. 'If you want someone to protect you, you have to trust them.'

'Perhaps. Sadly, Alexis is unavailable.'

She seemed to relax a little. Her shoulders rose and fell with a long, deep breath. How would she take the rest of the news?

'He's on the run. Your father alleges that he stole fifty thousand euros.'

'No!'

The colour drained from Thea's face till she was as pale as moonlight. She slumped against the wall. Was she going to faint?

Christo jumped up from the desk at the same moment Sergei moved towards her. She held up her hand, halting them both. Sergei stood down but remained within arm's reach. Thea's trembling fingers moved to touch the pendant at her throat and she seemed to compose herself.

'Alexis is no thief.' Her voice scraped the words out.

A hot throb of anger burned in his chest. He looked at Sergei. 'Excuse us.'

The bodyguard nodded acknowledgement and left the room.

Christo glared at Thea. 'You said the same of yourself.'

Her denial was futile in the face of his evidence.

'I think your professed skill at accumulating money is a myth, and that you stole it like I originally suspected. With the help of a complicit bodyguard.'

'You can think what you want.'

She chewed at her lip, teeth biting so hard she might draw blood. Mercifully the colour had returned to her cheeks, though she still used the wall as support.

'All you give me is lies,' Christo growled. 'One truth. That's all I ask. Tell me one deep, abiding truth about yourself.'

Thea's plump bottom lip quivered, then firmed. The hand fiddling with her necklace fell to her side, clenching in a tight fist. She pushed away from the wall, bringing her luscious body closer to his.

Every part of him stood on high alert. He didn't care that Sergei waited outside the door. He didn't care that Thea was a liar. He craved to slide his arm round her slender waist, to push her back against the wall and take her so hard the only word from her lips would be his name, screamed loud.

'A truth, Christo?'

She tossed her head. The soft chocolate waves of her hair swirled round her shoulders. Her mouth curled into a bitter smile as she placed her hand on his chest where it seared like a brand.

'I'm not very partial to ouzo.'

Then she stalked from the room with an exaggerated sway of her hips, slamming the door behind her.

Thea jogged away from the building which housed Christo's apartment. She took a route to Central Park in a steady rhythm, with Sergei following a discreet distance behind. New York rushed in its gritty, inexorable way around her. Every part vibrant, hustling and alive.

She should have been enthralled by this place—the city that never slept. Yet after five days here all Thea wanted to do was sleep. There was no way to ease the pressure winding inside her, tighter and harder. It crept up on her as she dressed. Tried to throttle her as she fastened around her throat the fine necklace her mother had given her as a child.

Alexis was on the run, and she couldn't help from this beautiful, blazing city. This place her mother had always wanted her to see.

Thea had once had childish dreams of coming here with someone she loved. Those dreams had died the day her mother had. Now she wanted none of it. The risk of losing her heart, and with it her freedom, was too high a price to pay.

Anyhow, Christo despised her. After that exchange in his office, the interminable silence on his plane, she had been left only with businesslike interactions before each function. Information so she knew who was coming, what to say.

It was preferable, all this sullen formality. Except when they were on show as a couple. Then he epitomised the perfect husband. Pretending to be interested, pretending to care. All those affectionate meaningless touches and still her treacherous body sang to every single one.

Those thoughts chased her. So Thea ran. Ran till the air burned in her lungs and she couldn't suck another breath. Ran till her heart thrashed in her chest as if to escape. She stopped at a tree, one hand gripping the rough bark. Retching from the exertion. And still she hadn't run far enough. From the people. The crowds. From herself. The feelings.

She folded at the waist, gasping for air. Her free hand was on her thigh, fingernails cutting into the screaming muscle. The cruel bite of pain helped. She'd focus on that. Wait till her heart stopped slamming like a battering ram at her ribs.

Still the air wouldn't come quickly enough, her lungs heaving. The clutch of panic grabbed tighter. Her vision blurred at the edges. She'd faint. She'd die. Here, in front of everyone.

Heavy footsteps thudded behind her. An arm under hers gave support. An urgent voice pierced the fog.

'Mrs Callas!'

Sergei.

She found her breath. Steadied it.

In for four. Hold. Out for eight. Repeat.

She moved to a seat somehow. Sat with her elbows on her knees. Head buzzing.

There was a water bottle. The murmur of words. Strange. Distant.

'Are you all right…? Do you need a doctor…? I've called Mr Callas.'

She sat up with a sharp intake of breath, hands trembling as her upside-down world righted itself.

'No!'

Sergei stepped back. He'd hardly broken sweat, whereas her skin was slick with it, stinging her eyes. Thea wiped at the hair sticking to her face. When was the last time she'd had an attack this bad?

She stood, legs on fire and shaking like a newborn lamb. 'I don't need Mr Callas. I'm going back to the apartment.' She tried to sound strong, but her voice cracked.

Soft rain fell as she walked, sprinkling over her skin. At the doors of the building she was welcomed by the ever-friendly doorman. Dripped water all over the marble floor of the lift to the penthouse, where Christo's apartment took up the whole level.

Sergei hovered close. 'Are you sure you're well?'

Panic, her old enemy, always followed her. Taunting from the shadows. She wouldn't let it win.

'I pushed myself a little hard.'

An ambush like today was a concern, because it normally heralded more attacks. But she'd fight back. Regain control.

'It was more than that,' Sergei said as the lift stopped at the top floor and they exited. He punched the key code to enter the apartment.

'Worried I'll die on your watch?'

'You might feel like you're dying, but I won't let that happen,' he said as he held the door open for her. 'I'll carry paper bags for next time.'

Thea shot a look over her shoulder. 'That won't be necessary.'

He shrugged and exchanged a concerned look with Anna, who'd rushed towards them. Sergei must have texted her.

'I'm fine. Really,' Thea said, as Anna opened her mouth to speak. 'I just need a shower and coffee.'

'I'll bring breakfast. You haven't been eating enough,' Anna chided.

Thea smiled. It felt stiff, unfamiliar, but if she faked it for long enough her smile might become reality. One day.

'In my room. Thank you.'

She went into her en suite bathroom. Discarded her sodden clothes and stood under the steaming shower as water pounded her skin, washing away the dark hand of fear threatening to strangle her.

She had to get help to Alexis. How dared her father accuse him of stealing the money she'd negotiated as part of her agreement to marry Christo?

But her father had lied and now her marriage was pointless.

Christo might help.

She silenced the inner voice. That would require trust she didn't have for another man who was using her for his own ends.

Thea turned off the water. Dried her now wrinkled skin and wrapped a robe tight around her body.

The food Anna had left held as much temptation as cardboard. So she lay on her side in the huge bed. Stared out at the drizzly view of New York sprawling below her. The place her mother would never see.

And, as much as she'd tried to outrun the feelings, now she let them overwhelm her. For Alexis. For this marriage. For that awful afternoon when she'd waited in the kitchen, clutching only her favourite doll and wearing her St Christopher medal for a safe journey. Waited for her mother to come through the small wooden side door and steal her away. Waited as the day had darkened and daylight had faded.

But the person she'd loved most in the world had never come. And the waiting had ended when her father found her and delivered the words which had changed her life for ever. *'Your mother's dead...'*

Thea curled tighter into a ball on her side, arms wrapped round her waist.

A shadowed reflection loomed in the window ahead of her. The prickle of awareness skittering along her spine announced that there was only one person it could be.

'Sergei says you were ill on your run.'

The voice was tight with concern. But Christo didn't care. He only wanted to ensure he inherited from his father. She was just a casualty along the way.

'I overexerted myself.'

'Sergei doesn't believe that.'

'I don't care what anyone believes.'

The bed dipped as Christo sat on the edge of the mattress. She didn't look at him. Only at the rain that beaded and slid down the window ahead of her.

'So you've made clear before. Would you like me to call a doctor?'

Thea shook her head. 'It's nothing. You shouldn't have interrupted your day.'

'Sergei called. I came.'

A cool hand rested on her forehead. She closed her eyes.

'No temperature...'

So few people cared about her. She could count them on one hand: Alexis, Elena. Anna and Sergei, perhaps, but they were paid to care, after all. Same as the servants at her father's home, who'd looked after her when her mother had left. And still, like the little girl she'd once been, she craved the caring with a bone-numbing ache.

'We have the dinner party tonight.' Christo's voice was gentle and soothing. 'I'll cancel it.'

'No, I'll be there as promised.'

Her voice quavered and caught. She cleared her throat. Stupid. To fall for these tiny scraps of kindness, tossed to her by a man who cared as little for her as her father did. Still, a yearning twisted in her stomach.

'Are you sure?' he asked.

'Yes.'

She turned to him. Sat up. Pretending for a little while longer. They were so close on the bed. Her dishevelled in her robe. Him in his immaculately tailored dark trousers. The fine herringbone weave of his white shirt. Close enough for her to catch the scent of his aftershave and that whispered undertone she recognised instantly. Something dark and primal. All Christo.

Heat bloomed inside her, unravelling the tight twist of fear. Smoothing it out till the only ripple left was a low, sultry pulse she tried to ignore. But harder to ignore was his mouth…so close. The sensual curve of his lower lip… The slight shadow of stubble grazing his jaw…

His eyes fixed on hers. Hazel rimmed with slate, soft with concern. She shouldn't crave this, but for once she wanted to pretend that Christo cared too. The ache of it twisted hard, till her eyes burned with tears she refused to shed.

Still, it must have shown on her face. He cupped her cheek, his palm hot against her skin. 'What's wrong?'

Christo was trying to peer inside her, and she couldn't allow him to see too much.

Perhaps she'd tell him why she felt this way. It was a truth. A *real* truth, as Christo had demanded. But she was so full to the brim with truths they threatened to choke her. Her mother leaving. Finding Alexis. The years of deprivation. Fighting to retain a part of herself when darkness threatened to devour her. She'd pasted so many false layers over her true self—one breach of the barrier and it would all fall apart. She couldn't risk it. Not for this man.

She closed her eyes to shut him out as he threaded his hands into the tangle of her hair. The warmth of his breath was close, so close. She might not be able to tell him anything, but she could allow herself to let go. For a moment. She was entitled to that at least, wasn't she?

'Thea…'

Her name was a whisper as his lips brushed hers. She didn't care any more about pushing him away. For once, all she cared about was succumbing to sensation. Forgetting the world was hard and real and taking pleasure for herself and damn the consequences. Losing herself and ignoring the fear of gilded cages and the trap of marriage, even one with a time frame as short as theirs.

She slid her hands to the back of his neck, into his dark hair…softer than she'd imagined for such a hard man. Pulling him closer, she pressed her lips to his. He deepened the kiss, his tongue gliding over hers as she relished the invasion.

She wanted all of him. Because now she didn't have to think—she could *feel*. The rasp of his growing stubble. The prickle of her scalp as his fingers tightened in her hair. His lips teasing, testing, as he eased her backwards onto the bed. The heavy weight of him as he lay over her and pressed her down, down into the soft covers.

Her legs fell open, cradling his hips between hers. The ridge of hardness at his groin notched into her with a delicious burn. She writhed under him, shifting restlessly as she tried to alleviate the ache there, losing herself in the erotic grind of their bodies. Her skin overheated till she felt desperate to tear her clothes away.

This was a flame only Christo could quench.

He was rocking against her. The tightness low inside her twisting tighter and harder. He tore at her robe, his breath mingling with hers as they panted and moved against each other. His searching fingers drifted over her breast, teasing at her nipple till heat seared between her thighs. She moaned, but his kiss trapped the sound.

Thea tore her mouth from his and gasped for air. 'Please... Please...'

She toyed with the buttons of his shirt. No thought other than having him naked and inside her, quelling the ache now at a fever pitch.

'I have you,' he murmured. 'I'll look after you.'

It wasn't enough. Her whole body screamed to be filled by him. She didn't care. Nothing mattered any more but this. His hips worked against hers. The edge of oblivion was close. So close. She wrapped her legs tight round him. Gripped his back and arched into him as he rolled her nipple between his fingers and kissed and kissed, his tongue delving into her mouth.

Then nothing.

Everything stopped.

Why? Why was he so still?

She groaned, and didn't care how frustrated, how desperate she sounded.

'Oh, no!'

Anna's voice?

Christo turned his head towards it as his hands gently closed her robe, his body still covering her.

'What do you want?' he growled.

Christo was coiled tight, but there was the slightest tremble through his huge frame, and she wasn't sure whether it was unsatisfied desire, or anger at being disturbed. She buried her head in the side of his neck to hide her face, breathing in the clean scent of him mingled with something musky and erotic. Desire and arousal…

'The breakfast plates. I'll—'

'Please leave.' The words were a hiss through his clenched teeth.

'I'm sorry…'

The clink of cutlery, shoes scuffing on carpet and then the snick of the door signalled Anna's departure.

And a return of Thea's common sense.

What had she been doing? All of this was evidence of how easily she could be ensnared. Her heart raced. Not in a way that was pleasant or spoke of passion, but thready and panicked.

'*Koukla mou,*' Christo said, stroking his thumbs over her jaw.

No, she couldn't do this. He still wanted her. His interest hadn't diminished and he remained hard and ready. But for her it was like being plunged into a stream of meltwater. She shifted and pushed. Because she couldn't be under him anymore.

He rolled from her as she sat up and tied her robe tight—too tight. How needy she'd been. He must leave. She could never allow him to see her like this again.

'Don't you need to be back at work?' She reached trembling fingers to her lips, which were tender and bee-stung from his kisses.

Christo raked his hand through his hair, a crease forming between his brows. 'I could stay.'

His eyes were hot on hers. The invitation in them, clear and tempting. Too much more and she'd burst into flames. But she couldn't—not now. Even though the memory of his touch, his hardness between her thighs, burned relentlessly.

Thea chewed the inside of her mouth. Clenched her hands into fists and let her nails bite the soft flesh of her palms. She mustn't forget the only reason she was here was the deal, and what her father had done to force her compliance.

It was nothing more than business. Her body had never been part of the bargain, no matter the ache at her core and how much every cell protested Christo's absence.

She shook her head. 'No. Go. Take over the world or whatever you plan on doing today.'

He hesitated, then stood. Still hard. The zip of his trousers was straining; his shirt was crushed. He looked delicious and disarrayed, like she'd never seen him before. Warmth coursed through her—a heady rush of power. *She'd* done that to him. This implacable man was now softened and less than perfect. Looking...human. Devastatingly handsome. Her husband.

But in the end it was all meaningless.

Christo took a step back, smiled, but something about it appeared stiff and brittle, not reaching his eyes. 'World domination isn't as entertaining in your absence.'

He leaned over, touched his lips to her forehead. Then he brushed a gentle hand over her hair, straightened and left the room.

As she curled back into herself Thea hated it that his last moment of tenderness caused a tear to slip down her cheek.

CHAPTER SEVEN

CHRISTO SAW OFF his dinner party guests. Exchanged crushing handshakes. Suffered pats on the back and the words, 'Give my regards to Hector.'

His father had always been the centre of any party. Splashing millions around in a way Christo never would. Yet he needed to secure the loyalty of these people if his plan to save Atlas was to succeed. To cement ties which would stand when Hector was gone.

There was so much work to do, and tonight, he still had another part to play. He'd be accompanying the men to an exclusive club. Without their wives. That suggestion by one of his guests had been telling in itself.

Perhaps Thea would share a coffee with him before he left? She'd been wary of him since he'd arrived home, earlier than expected, after leaving her looking so tumbled and wanton on her bed. His day of meetings had been shot to pieces because fantasies of Thea naked and himself buried deep inside her had consumed his every thought. Especially now he knew how they ignited together.

The same thoughts obviously hadn't plagued her. He could tell by the way she avoided his gaze, flitted away from him when he tried to get close. He couldn't abide that reticence. He wanted the fire, the passion. Her pleas for him to satisfy her ringing loud in his ears.

His hunger for her was something he longed to explore. Like the hills and valleys of her glorious body which so far he'd barely touched. Still, the sensible part of him cautioned that he must keep the distance he'd deliberately maintained till now. A challenging task when his hunger for her remained undiminished, despite the lies.

Although his broker had called, advising him that the

solar company she'd recommended was on its way to making him millions. So what she'd told him about her money-making abilities appeared true.

This dissonance in his picture of her unsettled him. She remained an enigma, and in his ordered world he hated puzzles.

The apartment was hushed and in near darkness as he walked towards the dining room to find her. Only the glow from the myriad candles on the long table seating twenty flickered in the room.

Christo hesitated near the door. Thea gleamed in the low lights. She was elegant and understated in black, yet she'd shone more brightly than any of the other women, with their colourful clothes and sparkling jewels. She drifted around the table, blowing out candle after candle. Their waxy smell thick in the air.

She stopped in front of the table's centre, her face illuminated in the golden light of a squat candle in the middle of an arrangement, which held a well of melted wax around its flame. She dipped the tip of her finger into it, blowing till the thin coating of wax hardened. Then she picked up the candle and tipped a stream of molten liquid onto her open palm.

Christo started forward, gut clenching hard. He should stop her. It must burn. Yet all he could do was watch, transfixed, as she toyed with the fire. Replacing the candle, Thea licked her fingers and pinched out the flame, then another, and another. Each one was extinguished with a quiet hiss.

He couldn't take any more.

She jumped as he stepped into the honeyed light. 'I thought you'd already left.'

He didn't miss the curl of her hand, closing over her wax-covered palm, as he strolled round the table towards her.

'I'm going soon,' he said, keeping his voice calm.

She stood like a cornered animal. Eyes wide, body stiff. He didn't want that. He wanted her soft and pliant and pleading to be sated.

'What were you doing?'

'Putting out the candles.'

Thea was the expert at never really answering a question. Why had she mastered that skill? He could ask, but chose not to. He didn't think she'd tell him even if he did.

'You'll burn yourself.'

'I never have before.'

And there was the tiny truth he'd longed for—though he wasn't sure what it meant. He searched her face for any hint. Her expression gave him nothing, but she looked pale. Like a Technicolor picture fading to sepia, all the vibrancy leached from her. Unlike when they'd kissed this morning. Then, she'd glowed.

'I wanted to thank you for tonight,' he said.

She had an innate sense for the role of gracious hostess, charming men and women alike. For that he was indebted to her.

'There's no need. I had a job to do.'

How selfish he'd been. He should have rescheduled the party, as he'd offered. A splinter of concern pricked at him. She'd only toyed with her dinner tonight, and he noticed her dress hung loosely on her curves.

'You aren't well. Don't think I haven't appreciated your efforts.'

'I'm used to it. It's little different from my father's demands.'

He hated the comparison to her father. Just as he hated the dull, dead tone to her voice and the lack of light in her eyes. Where had all her flash and fire gone?

'I thought you might like to share a coffee with me before I leave.'

Perhaps he could forgo his obligations for one night. Instead coax Thea to indulge in the pleasure of burning together once more.

She cocked her head, narrowed her gaze. In that moment she made him feel like a schoolboy, asking out his first date.

He had an insane desire to peer down at his shoes and scuff them on the carpet.

'Where are you headed?' she asked, her face bland and unreadable.

Another request from him left unanswered.

'We're meeting at someone's club.'

Somewhere that was by invitation only. Discreet. Where morals could be compromised or forgotten. The sort of place he despised.

The prospect of spending time there exhausted him. At least being newly married he could reject the menu he'd be offered there without anyone questioning it. Tonight would cost him only money, not his soul. All he had to do was keep his father's associates happy and try to recover what Hector had wrecked—ensure the upcoming celebration of Atlas Shipping's seventy-fifth year didn't become a wake instead.

'Ah. More *business*.'

He didn't miss the raised eyebrow, her loaded tone. He could show her again how they combusted together. *Then* she'd ask him to stay.

Christo took a step forward. Thea stepped back, eyes wary. He hesitated. She didn't desire this like he did. So he couldn't ignore his gentlemen guests' request to take tonight's party elsewhere.

'Sadly,' he said, and meant it. But he knew too well when he wasn't wanted.

'I won't keep you from your fun.' She gave a wan smile. 'I'm tired. I want to go to bed.'

Thea blew out the last candle, plunging the room into darkness. He watched as she walked down the hall, slender fingers still clenched over her wax-encrusted palm.

Thea sat up with a jolt, heart pounding, a slick ache between her thighs. She pushed her palms into her eyes and rubbed till bright flashes burst behind her lids.

She was trying and failing, to scrub away a dream of she

and Christo entwined. Touching. Tasting. Indulging in her sleep, what she wouldn't take for herself when awake. The vestiges of desire clung, making her nipples hard knots, abrading even under the soft fabric of her top.

She could ease the ache herself. It wouldn't take much—not the way she felt…

No. Christo would remain off-limits in both fantasy and reality. It was safer that way.

She picked up her phone to check the time, noticed the message alert flashing bright. Two in the morning, meaning it was about eight in the morning at home in Athens. A message. *Alexis.* Could it be?

Thea grappled with the handset. Fumbled her password twice before succeeding.

Her heart leapt for a moment, then her shoulders dropped as she saw the name. Not Alexis. Demetri.

You're taking your time.

He was referring to the information her father had demanded about Christo's business. She wanted no part of this, or their shady schemes. Whatever information her father and Demetri requested, it wasn't for honest reasons.

Thea typed her reply. Damn her clumsy, trembling fingers.

Go to hell.

A response pinged back.

Will see Alexis there first if you don't get what we want.

She swallowed the tight ball closing her throat. There it was. The threat. The reason they'd reported him to the police. Her fault—again.

She tossed her phone onto the bed. Choked back a sob. She had no way of easing the emotional pain threatening to crack her. The crushing pressure that made her want to scratch at her skin, to flay it from her body till she bled.

Not even the bright burn of that candle wax had diminished the relentless ache. Thea rubbed at her palm, still tingling after all these hours. What a foolish move that had been—especially with Christo witnessing her weakness. She recognised that moment earlier for what it had evidenced. Desperation. Where was all her caution, her control?

She curled into a ball on the bed for a few moments and then rose, refusing to lie there and feel sorry for herself. She needed to do something—anything to keep moving, give herself time to think.

Her stomach griped with the twin agony of nerves and hunger pangs, punishing her for not having eaten enough. That was as good a motivation as any.

She traipsed down the unlit hall towards the kitchen. The astonishing New York skyline glittered through every window, lighting up the space in its silvery glow. She glanced over the view, unmoved.

Once at the refrigerator, she grabbed some bread, cheese and milk—ate in the comforting darkness because she didn't care what she put into her stomach so long as that crippling inertia didn't steal over her again.

The apartment lay silent. Sergei and Anna were sensibly asleep. Christo was still out. It was better that she didn't see him. Her emotions regarding the man were a tangle she couldn't sort through. Simpler to avoid it. Anyhow, they'd be returning to Greece soon. Back to the numbing routine of Christo working long hours and her futile efforts to find Alexis.

She needed someone with different skills. Perhaps Sergei would help? Anna had told her he'd been in the Special

Forces in his home country. But how to convince a man as immovable as a hunk of concrete to assist her?

Thea was contemplating any number of ways to approach Sergei on the way back to her room. No option stood out. But as she padded down the hallway noises stopped her. A rustle, a smothered giggle...

She moved towards the sound, beckoned by the soft, golden glow coming from the direction of Christo's study. The door was slightly ajar. She heard whispers. Male and female. The clatter of pens falling. She walked faster. Heart pounding. Drawn towards the light with a sense of dread.

She's heard enough to recognise that murmured intimacies were being exchanged. They didn't have a real marriage, but surely Christo wouldn't bring someone back here? After he'd touched her? So clearly displayed his desire? Though she knew men lied about fidelity all the time. Men like her father. And where else would Christo go if he didn't want to be caught and their marriage exposed as a fraud?

She didn't understand why the thought seized her with a sense of humiliation as she approached the door.

She heard a breathy sigh, a male groan—*'Agapi mou...'*— and her humiliation exploded in a screaming hot conflagration which roared through her. She couldn't see anything through the crack of the door, but to *hell* with Christo bringing someone to the apartment after demanding that theirs must appear like a real marriage in all respects. How *dared* he? After kissing her? Making her *feel*?

She flung the door back. Stormed in. Wild. Not caring what she'd find.

Wide eyes. Gasps of shock. The scramble of two people caught out. Anna was on Christo's desk, her hair a tumbled mess, her skirt hitched high on her thighs. And Sergei was standing there. Stripped to the waist.

'Mrs Callas—I can explain,' Sergei said as Anna clutched at her open blouse.

Thea held up her hand to stop him. What she'd interrupted had only just started. Relief washed over her like a warm shower—to be quickly replaced by a calculated resolve.

Sergei didn't attempt more excuses, only glanced down at Anna, cupped her jaw in what seemed like a moment of reassurance. But that look… Tight with concern and brimming with something else. Softness, intent… She recognised it instantly. *Love.*

In that moment Thea was assailed by two thoughts. The first was a terrifying craving for Christo to look at her with the same expression Sergei had given Anna. The second was the realisation that she now had the means to make her bodyguard do anything she desired.

'No need for explanations,' she said, her voice firm and hard. 'We won't mention this again. But I want you to find Alexis Anastos for me. And, Sergei…? You will *not* tell Mr Callas.'

CHAPTER EIGHT

'IF HE'S STILL in Greece he remains well hidden, even though his bank accounts are frozen.'

Thea stiffened at the sound of Sergei's voice as he approached her where she sat on the private terrace under an ancient olive tree. She put down her coffee. The dappled morning light shifted over an uneaten breakfast. Despite Sergei's efforts since they'd returned to Athens, Alexis hadn't been found. Reason told her to remain calm. But the clawing fear that he was out there alone, without money or help, tore in her abdomen.

'Thank you,' she said, as Sergei positioned himself at the end of the table. 'Do you think he might have left the country?'

'Anything's possible.'

She read between his words. Crossing borders illegally cost money. And right now Alexis had nothing. That meant he needed her help.

'Keep looking.'

Sergei cleared his throat. 'I'm not comfortable about this.'

She picked up her coffee and took a long sip, peering at him over the rim of the cup. They'd had this discussion many times before Sergei had finally agreed to help her.

'I wasn't comfortable about finding you half-naked in my husband's office. Let's both bear it as best we can—for Anna's sake.'

His expression didn't change. He stood inhumanly still, legs apart, hands behind his back, staring blankly over her head. 'Of course.'

'Remember—I'll keep your secrets if you keep mine.'

Thea loathed this. Loathed the things she'd said to garner his cooperation. It was clear he'd do anything to protect the woman he loved, so that was whose job she'd threatened. He didn't need to know she'd never tell Christo. In fact Anna was turning into more of a friend than an employee. But Thea was trying to protect someone *she* loved too. And she'd go to any lengths—just like Sergei would.

'Excellent.' She slid a piece of paper towards him. 'Now that's settled, today I want to go here.'

That simple act, making her request, led to the slow unknotting of the muscles in her neck. Sergei couldn't object, and here was a way to relieve some of the tension winding her so tight she felt her bones were bound to splinter.

Sergei picked up the note, looked at it, at her and then back at the note. A muscle ticked in his cheek. 'Mr Callas was specific in his instructions when he engaged me, and—'

'Again, there's no need for Christo to know.' Anger bubbled inside her, hot and thick. Sergei's job wasn't to keep her safe. Christo had merely subcontracted the role of her nanny and jailer because he couldn't be bothered doing it himself.

'I can keep the fact I'm looking for someone behind Mr Callas's back a secret. But...' He held up the scrap of paper with a name and address on it between his fingers, hissing his words through gritted teeth. 'A tattoo?'

'Your job is to keep to our agreement. Mine's to deal with Christo.' She narrowed her eyes. 'Every action has consequences. Take responsibility for yours and let me worry about my own.'

Sergei looked heavenward and muttered something. It might have been a curse, or even a prayer. She waited for him to finish.

'Do you know where this place is?' she asked.

'Yes.' He screwed up the piece of paper and stuffed it into his trouser pocket. 'It's where I get mine. Shall I call for the car now?'

She raised her cup to him in a toast. 'Perfect.'

They drove to the tattoo parlour without speaking. Sergei was taciturn at the best of times. Today his silence seemed ominous. As they parked, she tried not to think about how Christo would feel, or why his good opinion mattered.

Sergei scanned the narrow back street. After a short while he opened her door and ushered her out. 'Would you like me to come in and hold your hand?' His words were dry as alum.

She patted his rock-solid forearm. 'I bet I have more tattoos than you.'

He raised an eyebrow. 'I doubt it. Perhaps when you're done we could compare?'

Thea laughed. His sense of humour was unexpected. She saw why Anna liked him. 'Now, how would we explain *that* scene to Mr Callas?'

Sergei grunted in reply as they walked into the bright white waiting room. He took his place, standing to attention near the door.

Thea was invited through by a large man with more ink than bare skin. Not her usual artist, but it didn't matter. She riffled through a portfolio of his work. He appeared skilled. Anyway, she knew what she wanted. She couldn't turn back now. The need for it slid through her veins like a drug.

She took off her shirt, felt her heartbeat slowing to a sleepy rhythm.

The man moved behind her. '*Nice*. And you want another where?'

'At the end. Follow what I designed with Marco last time. Make sure it stays below the bra line.'

She lay forward, relaxing as the man prepared. Calm spread over her at the familiar routine, soft and cocooning as a goose down quilt. *This* was her reward. For the forced marriage. For every hurt. No matter how hard people tried to shape her into their own image, no one could steal the essence of her. Here was her proof—in the secrets scribed on her body.

'Ready?' the man asked.

'Yes.' It was almost a sigh of relief. She smiled and closed her eyes as the needle bit into her skin.

Something had changed. Thea seemed happier. There was a sense of peace about her now, as they sat down to breakfast. She glowed with a mysterious, ethereal kind of beauty that tugged at him.

Christo had seen that look in women who were pregnant, the secret joy. Strange imagining that with her when it was impossible. Yet still the thought trickled through him with a slide of warmth.

Rather than picking at the food, as she'd done since New York, today she ate a large meal. It pleased him in an inexplicable way to see her looking more settled. He wasn't sure why he cared. Yet he felt a deep satisfaction in her new-found happiness.

A partnership. That was how their relationship had begun to feel. Something he'd never expected when he'd checked off the list of things he must do to ensure Atlas's safety.

What would it be like to have a true partnership? A woman in his mind, his bed, his heart?

He looked over the table at his wife. Strange how he'd never thought he'd ever be married. Especially now there was an odd companionship in their forced togetherness. Some comfort in having another person in his home who might learn to care, as he was learning.

Thea. A luminous mystery…so much of her hidden. The desire to unlock her secrets, stuck under his skin. To inflame the passion which kindled between them. No games. No reining anything in. Both of them allowed free flight to every fantasy.

He'd felt in New York how it would be, with the force of a blow. All his desires exploding into life in the bright burst that was Thea.

She looked at him and smiled, a soft tilt to her lips. The

allure of her rushed through him, and a clutch of need gripped him in a way he'd never felt.

'There are some more people you'll meet at the party,' he said, trying to ignore the pull that drew him to her.

Thea sipped a coffee, her lipstick leaving a pale pink stain on the cup. 'Who are they and what should I know?'

'More business contacts.'

'What about friends?'

'No.'

A faint frown marred her brow. 'Do you have any?' she said, like it was a surprise to her that he could be close to anyone.

Christo hesitated. Thea was nearer to the truth than she realised. But why did he feel the need to explain? They had a business deal. He would simply dictate the terms and she'd do what he wanted, without the need to bare his soul. Yet that look of hers judged him, as lethal as a stab to the heart.

'Of course.'

Except he spent all his time bolstering Atlas. Nothing else had mattered for longer than he remembered. Including other people. He scrubbed his hands over his face, every part of him weary.

She shrugged. 'Tell me what I need to know and I'll be ready.'

Thea always assimilated the information he gave her and used it in the most gracious of ways. Making every person she met feel special, as if they were old friends. There was strength in her. She didn't want this, yet she carried on with persistence and dedication. And that part of her glowed more brightly than mere beauty ever could, lighting the darkest places of him.

'Tonight, perhaps we could have dinner on the terrace and discuss it.' There, under the olive trees, seemed to be her favourite place.

He smiled. Thea smiled back and the warmth of it filled him to overflowing.

'I'd love to.'

She sounded genuinely pleased. He contemplated staying home from work today. Taking time away from shoring up support for Atlas and spending it here. With her.

A low pulse picked up a throbbing tempo in his gut. He was sure they could find something pleasurable to do together...

'Mr Callas?'

His thoughts were interrupted by Anna.

'Your car's here.'

Christo's shoulders sagged. More work. Stitching together the gaping holes left by his father. But he'd win this battle and release Atlas from its debts. Release Thea in the process. Yet something about that prospect sat bitter in his mouth.

He stood. Anna was looking on, so he kissed Thea on the lips. Her rich scent curled into him and something deep inside clenched with need. Better he leave for work than risk exploring that hunger.

As he passed Thea, he noticed a vivid red mark on the back of her white blouse. 'You've blood on your shirt.'

Thea lifted her head, a look of concern flickering over her face before disappearing. Her features reverted to a blank calm. 'I had a bite. It must have been bigger than I realised.'

She smiled again, but this one was flat and lifeless.

'Perhaps someone should take a look?'

She rolled her eyes. 'It's nothing. A mosquito bite, and I scratched too hard.'

He accepted her explanation reluctantly. After all she was an adult, could look after herself.

'Now, go,' she said, with a flick of her hand, her engagement ring twinkling in the fresh morning light. 'Sergei can look after me. That's why you hired him, isn't it?'

She turned back to her breakfast and he felt strangely dismissed.

* * *

An amateur mistake, wearing white. Thea stormed into her room and tore off her shirt, throwing it on the dresser. She should have been more careful. Yet she wasn't thinking clearly, being ruled by emotion. It was causing her to make stupid mistakes.

She reached behind her, peeled off the dressing and turned to look in the mirror. Okay, more bleeding than she'd had before, but not infected—at least she didn't think so. This tattoo hurt more than usual too, but that was bound to be its position on her spine.

She peered over her shoulder at the flock of birds soaring across her back, showing that no matter how many people tried to cage her, in the end she'd be free.

Christo couldn't hold her. Nor could her father. They'd all try, but she'd slip through the bars one day and fly away for ever. Until then she'd add bird after bird. Marks to commemorate each insult as a reminder that her time would come.

Thea grappled with the dressing, twisting awkwardly as she tried to replace it. Only a few days and the tattoo would heal. She'd just be more careful. Perhaps she should wear a black shirt?

Then in the mirror she saw a movement. *Christo.* Watching with fury twisting ugly across his features.

'What the hell is this?'

She snatched up her shirt. Clutched it to her chest. And all the simmering feelings bubbled and boiled and spilled over in a scalding flood.

'Get out!' Her composure was gone in a torrent of white-hot anger. She trembled as it burned through her. 'You've no right to be in here.'

'I have every right. This is my house.' He towered in the doorway. Jaw hard. Mouth stretched in a thin, brutal line. 'You'll explain this.'

'It's my body. I can do what I like with it.'

Christo's lip curled into a sneer. 'What else have you been doing with it when my back's been turned?'

'I'm sure your imagination can conjure any number of horrors.'

The cool air of the room chilled her overheated skin. Or perhaps it was the cold rage in Christo's eyes. She felt too exposed, with the shirt held in front of her and his icy gaze flicking to her tattoos reflected in the mirror behind.

'And you will document each one for me,' he said. 'My study. One hour.'

Christo hadn't thought himself a fool for years—not since childhood. Not since he'd believed his parents' false promises time and again, till he'd stopped believing anything. Yet here Thea was, sitting in front of him, her whole presence mocking as if he was one.

He'd gone to check on her. Genuinely worried. And what had he found? Evidence of betrayal. Lies. People always told lies. Especially those you allowed close to you. Never again.

It was clear she didn't care. Leaning back in the chair opposite, arms crossed, a victorious gleam in her eye. That was why she'd looked so happy—because she'd thought she'd won.

It might not be a real marriage, but he'd made vows and he'd keep them till the end. He'd expected the same of her.

Where to begin when the rage scorched through him? He searched for the chill usually running in his veins. *She* did this to him—made him unreasonable. And he was usually a reasonable man.

'Sergei's employment has been terminated.'

'That's unfair. I want you to reinstate him. He's an excellent bodyguard.'

'He told me everything.'

Actually, Sergei had only admitted to an error of judgement—trying to protect Thea's shattered honour, no doubt. But Christo knew there was little that would make a consummate professional like Sergei forget where his allegiances lay. An illicit affair with his employer's beautiful young wife was the only explanation.

But Christo wanted the truth from Thea's lips, not Sergei's. The truth that she hadn't stuck to their bargain of fidelity, that she was like his parents. An opportunistic liar.

As he stared her down, myriad emotions flickered across her face. It was like watching a movie on fast forward. Surprise, disbelief, sorrow. Until she plastered on her usual smooth veneer of calm.

'Love can make a man do uncharacteristic things. Of course you don't believe in love, so you would never know.'

Christo gritted his teeth. His suspicions were right. A pain knifed him deep inside, causing an aching wound to his soul. He'd craved her. Kissed her. And for what? Merely to repeat Hector's mistakes?

'You're so like your father.'

Damn his mother's words—the last she'd spoken to him. They hadn't been meant as a compliment.

He cast them into the wasteland of his memory. They had no place here. He'd married Thea for convenience, not love. So why did evidence of her betrayal tear to the very heart of him?

He gripped the arms of his chair till his nails bit into the leather. 'I'm sure you're easy to love when you want to get your own way.'

The cool calm thawed and her eyes widened a fraction. Triumph leapt inside him, a bitter white-hot flame. He'd caught her out.

'You think…? Me?'

She sounded incredulous—another act.

'That I'd trade myself to Sergei to get what I want? I may be many things, but I'd never do that.'

'Don't lie to me.' Christo flew from his chair, hands trembling. Every part of him was too hot, too tight for his suit. He tore off his tie before it choked him. 'I won't be taken for a fool like my father!'

Turning a blind eye to his wife's outrageous behaviour. Ignoring it till she ran off with her latest lover. Christo thought he'd avoided his genetics, the weakness allowing him to be conned by women. He had believed Thea was more. But glorious curves and luscious kisses had caused him to look past the truth of another duplicitous female.

'I'm not lying. Even though you've done nothing to earn my trust.'

He placed his hands on the desktop and leaned forward. Thea didn't move, her expression placid, as if she'd done nothing wrong at all.

'Sergei was protective,' he hissed. 'There's only one reason a man behaves that way!'

She laughed at him—a cold jeer. It was the way his father had been laughed at for years by his mother in the charade of their marriage.

'As you know so well, being the great protector that you are.'

He refused to be mocked. 'How quickly you move on from one man to the next. I hope using Sergei was worth it to get back at me. What happened? Did you seduce him when you realised Alexis was unavailable?'

Thea leapt from her seat, chest heaving. 'Alexis is my *brother*!'

A dreadful quiet fell in the room, taking on a life of its own. Heavy, oppressive, punctuated by Thea's ragged breaths. A clock on the wall ticked seconds in an ominous rhythm.

'He was like the brother I should have had.'

She only had one brother. Didn't she?

More lies.

'You want to know why I did this?' she asked.

Thea grabbed the bottom of her shirt and tore, buttons scattering as she hurled the ruined fabric to the floor, then whipped round, displaying her back. Christo stared at the birds sweeping across her skin, at the spidery detail of the feathers in their vivid colours.

'The first, I was eighteen. For all the times my father prevented me from seeing my mother. For the way she begged the staff to allow her to visit her little girl. I learned then the value of secrets and lies. This is a reminder of the sacrifices she made. How she fought to be free.'

The birds looked joyous as they twisted their way from the slender curve of her waist across her lower back and up her spine. Christo counted. Nine. Nine bluebirds.

'The one in the middle—the largest—it hurt the most. But not as much as what I did to earn it. Demetri promised me to one of his business associates. To close a deal.'

Christo froze in horror. *No.*

'Luckily the man desired a "compliant" woman,' she spat, 'not one who'd fight. So I remained untouched. Demetri wasn't so forgiving. He always enjoyed hurting little girls.'

'But your father...' Surely he should have protected her?

She gave a mirthless laugh. She was still facing away from him, hands now defiantly planted on her hips, her nails digging into her flesh.

'My father didn't need his fists to make an impression. He'd take my phone—prevent my contact with the outside world to ensure compliance. I thought I'd go mad at times. In the end I behaved. Or he thought I did.'

He couldn't stand here and let her continue baring herself like this. 'Thea. Stop.' The words were rough as ground glass in his throat.

She shot a look behind her. 'Oh, please... You wanted to know and I'm keen to enlighten you. This bird, at my side...'

She catalogued a litany of deprivations. Too many for someone so young. He wanted to rage. To tear her family apart on her behalf. To *fix* this.

'But this last one. This one is all for *you*, Christo, my

beloved husband. When I told my father I wouldn't marry you Demetri stepped in to convince me. Alexis and Demetri fought. Then the police...'

She stopped. Slumped a little. Her shoulders rose and fell. Then she straightened.

'That's when my father discovered who Alexis was. He said he'd go to jail for assault unless I married you.' Her voice broke and trembled.

He wanted to reach for her. Hold her. Make it better, somehow. But the painful truth of their deal and what it had cost her was etched on her back, red and angry-looking. His fault and his shame.

The realisation sat leaden in his stomach.

'And you think I used my body, used Sergei, to get him to do what I wanted?'

She turned, bared to him apart from her bra. Christo couldn't keep his gaze from her devastated eyes.

'He doesn't deserve to be fired for doing what a good man should. Yes, Sergei's protecting the one he loves—but it's not me. I just blackmailed him into doing what I wanted.'

Defiant, she bent down for her shirt and shrugged it over her shoulders as she made for the door. When she reached it, she stopped.

'I've learned that blackmail is a blunt but effective instrument. As you know too well, being so good at it yourself.'

She left the room, clicking the door softly behind her.

The sound held more quiet horror than if she'd slammed it in his face.

Christo stood outside Thea's room, a bundle of papers in his hand. Even though he was the last person she'd want to see, he couldn't leave her alone. Not after what she'd disclosed. He wanted to prove to Thea that he wasn't like Tito or Demetri, that he could be trusted.

He took a steadying breath and tapped on the door, trying to ensure it sounded like a request to enter, not a demand. If she wanted her space he'd give it to her, but there were things that had to be said.

When there was no reply he turned the handle. Thea sat on her bed, leaning forward. She hadn't changed out of her ruined shirt, which still hung open. Her hands were clenched into rigid fists on her thighs.

He eased into the room.

She didn't look at him. Eyes fixed to the floor.

'I have the papers I promised,' he said, crouching down in front of her. 'Our settlement for when my father dies... the divorce. If you sign them, they'll be filed as soon as the will takes effect.'

'Do you have a pen?' Thea's voice was the barest whisper.

'You should read them first.'

'I don't care. I want nothing of yours.'

He handed her the sheaf of documents, which she glanced through. Then he drew a pen from his pocket. She took it and scrawled her name on the last page. His gut roiled as she signed, in a feeling of loss, a regret he had no right to have when for him, relationships had no permanence.

She thrust the documents at him, the papers quavering in her hand. 'Fill in what you need to when the time comes.'

Christo took them from her, dropped them on the floor beside him. 'No one should have gone through what you have.'

'And you care? I'm just a means to your end.'

Her fingers clenched tight again. He knew what she was doing now. Castigated himself for not realising before.

He took her hands in his. Stroked his thumbs over the blanched knuckles, absorbing the tremble running through her. She relaxed a fraction. He opened her fingers. Her nails had scored red crescents into her palms. He circled his thumbs over the livid marks, trying to smooth them away.

'You hurt yourself...'

Her eyes flicked to him. They were red-rimmed, her face flushed.

'This, the candles, the tattoos...'

He continued soothing her palms. Her hands burning hot under his thumbs.

'Not the tattoos. They're a reminder.'

'Of things you should never have experienced. If I'd known—'

'You wouldn't have done anything differently.'

Sunlight flooded in through the window behind her. It was such a glorious blue-sky day outside, and yet she spoke truths that broke a storm inside him.

Her accusation was right. He would have done anything to save Atlas Shipping. The knowledge sat heavy on his chest, making it tight and hard to breathe.

He couldn't change the past, but he could help with the present. 'Tell me about Alexis.'

The tremble in her body intensified, as if she was barely holding herself together. He steadied her hands between his.

'He's my half-brother,' she whispered, as if she were disclosing some terrible secret.

'And your father didn't know about him?'

Thea lifted her head, looked at him straight on. She chewed on her bottom lip, which quivered under her teeth.

'My parents were promised to each other from birth—an arrangement to merge two families' wealth. But my mother fell in love with someone else. At seventeen, she had Alexis. He was taken away. Adopted. My father still married her. He was only interested in the money he'd gain from it.'

Thea seemed so tired and worn down, with no fight left in her. As if it was an effort for her not to curl into herself and disappear.

'How did Alexis become your bodyguard?' asked Christo.

'My mother spent half her life trying to find him. When

she did, she told him he had a little sister. He said he'd find a way to look after me.'

She stopped. Took a shuddering breath. Christo squeezed her hands in reassurance.

'He worked in security. A position became vacant in my father's home. He applied. When he finally told me who he was it was like life began again.'

Thea sat up, pulling her hands from his. She wrapped her open shirt around her, hugging herself.

'The theft...it's a lie. When I agreed to marry you, I negotiated some money. Fifty thousand euros. Alexis was supposed to leave the country. Start again. But I couldn't save him.'

She dropped her head, toying with her engagement ring—another symbol of her failed efforts to protect her brother.

Christo's heart ached for her. She blamed herself, and yet Thea's only failure was in trusting that her father and Demetri would keep their side of the bargain.

'Do you know where he is?'

She shook her head. 'Sergei's been looking.'

He understood the blackmail now. The last resort for a desperate woman.

'He doesn't have my resources. I'll engage Raul's company. If anyone can find him, Raul can.'

Her eyelids fluttered shut. She clasped her hands as if giving a silent prayer. 'Thank you.'

He stood. Thea's trembling had turned into a shiver which racked her body. Her face and chest were flushed red. Christo reached out to cup her cheek. She burned.

'You're not well,' he said.

She tried to wave him away, but it seemed as if she was having trouble raising her arm. He pulled his phone from his pocket and called his doctor. Demanded he come to the house within the hour.

'I only need rest,' she said.

The slightest nudge and she'd collapse to the bed. He was sure of it. 'Then lie down…sleep a while,' he murmured.

Thea eased onto the pillows with no argument, curling on her side. Christo covered her with a blanket, tucking it tight around her as her teeth chattered.

His concern escalated. 'The doctor will be here soon.' Whilst he was no expert, her tattoo looked too pink. He only hoped she'd been looking after it as she should.

She stared at him, eyes glazed.

'I'm sorry,' he said. 'If there was any way this could have been different…'

He stroked her hair and Thea's fever-bright eyes drifted shut. Her breathing slowed in the rhythm of sleep. He pulled over a chair and sat next to the bed.

And as he watched her fitful rest he made a promise to do everything in his power to ensure Alexis's safety and to punish Tito and Demetri for what they'd done to her.

CHAPTER NINE

THEA WALKED INTO her bedroom and flopped into a chair, escaping the chaos downstairs. A flurry of party planners had transformed the huge lounge and entertainment area into a sumptuous ballroom for the evening. The home's modern lines had been draped and swathed until they mimicked the art deco opulence of the *Queen Mary*—the perfect setting for Atlas Shipping's anniversary celebrations.

She checked her watch. In a few short hours the party would begin—Christo's crowning achievement, where she'd be expected to glitter and shine. Even now a shaky kind of heat trembled through her. But this wasn't a hangover from the illness. It was something else altogether.

She'd taken a week to recover fully from what the doctor had assured Christo was a virus, and not an infected tattoo. After three days of being confined to her sickbed she'd risen to find that on the surface everything had returned to normal. Anna fussed about her assiduously. Sergei returned to work, taciturn as ever. The sun still rose, the night still fell, she ate, she slept...but *everything* was different.

It had changed as the fever racked her body. Christo's voice had grounded her, soothing as the cool run of a mountain stream. Each time she'd woken in those days, he'd been there, eyes stormy green and intent, dark stubble shading his jaw.

She suspected he hadn't left her bedside throughout her brief incapacitation. His gentle touches to check her temperature, to reassure, had melted her bones and left her wanting. Now all she craved was the soft lilt of his voice and his masculine touch. Because somehow what she'd shared with him had changed everything.

She walked into her dressing room, pulled out the gown

she planned to wear that night and laid it on the bed. The slither of fear snaked through her veins. Christo had warned her that Tito and Demetri were coming. Here, to this home, where she'd finally found some measure of comfort and safety.

This place…they'd taint it. She shivered. Why had Christo invited them when he knew what they'd done to her? He'd promised her there was good reason, just as he'd promised to protect her. If only she could find the means within herself to trust him…

'Mrs Callas?'

Thea looked up as Anna walked into the room, clutching an armful of boxes. 'I thought I told you to call me Thea.'

Anna smiled, bouncing on her toes. She seemed so happy—glowing. No more the shy woman Thea had first met. Obviously her relationship with Sergei was going well.

Was that what love could do to a person? Since it wasn't something she expected for herself, best not to muse on that.

'These are from Mr Callas,' Anna said in a breathless kind of way as she placed the packages on the bed.

Thea plucked a card from under the outrageous silver bow on the largest box, opened the envelope and read Christo's bold script.

Wear these tonight.

She glanced at her choice of dress for the evening, lying on the bed. A floor-length sheath. Black. Restrained and classical. Other women might compete to outdo each other. Not her.

Though curiosity made her fingers itch. What had Christo bought? It wouldn't hurt to look at what he'd chosen, would it?

She picked up the smallest box, stroking over the soft blue velvet. Jewellery? She eased the lid open and her hand flew to her mouth as the exposed contents glittered under the lights. Earrings. A twinkling confection of rubies and diamonds.

Thea lifted one and the chandelier fall of it trembled in her grasp. She couldn't help it. Slipped them into her ears and turned to the mirror. The flash of gems dangled low.

Anna gasped. 'They're beautiful. Like drops of blood and tears.'

'Tears?' Thea's voice cracked as she said it.

'Happy tears,' Anna said. 'Why wouldn't a woman be happy with a gift like that?'

Because it was too much.

And yet there was more.

Thea reached for the large box, tugging at the ends of the perfect bow holding it closed. Inside lay a garment of vivid red. She eased it from the folds of white tissue. Now it was her turn to gasp. A halter neck evening dress lined with satiny carmine silk lay inside. The whole of it was beaded, and it sparkled in a way that matched the earrings.

'I've never seen anything like it...' Anna whispered.

But Thea had observed what Anna hadn't. The back of the dress plunged. When it was on, it would leave her exposed.

Heart pounding, she flung it onto the bed as if the fabric had burned her. How could Christo demand she wear this? Even with her hair long and free, as she'd planned, her tattoos would be on view.

Heat flushed her cheeks. Did he intend to humiliate her?

Anna's voice intruded. 'The last box, Mrs... Thea?'

Strappy sandals to match the dress and earrings. Perfection in gold, adorned with red and clear jewels.

'Aren't you going to try them on?' Anna asked.

'I don't know if I should...'

'You must.' Anna planted her hands on her hips. 'What man doesn't want to show off his beautiful wife?'

Was that it? Surely not.

She glanced back at the dress, discarded on the bed.

Like nothing she'd ever owned. Brand-new. Couture. All hers. She fingered the exquisite fabric, soft, yet heavy in her hands.

Anna grabbed the black dress from the bed and went to the walk-in wardrobe.

Thea took a deep breath and began unbuttoning her blouse. She'd do this—then refuse the gift and return to her first choice.

She stepped into the gown. The silk lining slipped cool and seductive against her skin. She sat on the bed and toed into the shoes before rising. Beaded lace fell heavy against her.

Anna returned to the room, eyes wide. 'You're going to take everyone's breath away.'

Thea walked to the full-length mirror. Lace of blood-coloured perfection slid across her body. A dress meant to display a woman's shape. It flared at the bottom, so when she walked the lower half swished, beads glittering with every footstep. She turned and cast an eye over her shoulder. The back plunged tantalisingly low, but not indecently, framing the birds which soared over her spine.

Why had he chosen this? She couldn't wear it. Even though the fabric sang against her skin.

Thea walked back to her wardrobe with Anna trailing behind. She'd wear the dress she'd picked earlier. It wasn't showy, like this one, which allowed all her private wounds to be displayed.

'What beautiful tattoos,' Anna said quietly. 'So real... like they're ready to fly away.'

'Thank you.' Thea flicked through the hangers, looking for her black gown. Where had Anna hidden it? 'But I usually keep them covered. I can't wear this dress.'

'Why hide them?' Anna looked bemused. 'Mr Callas knows you have them, and he chose this dress for you—so he doesn't care.'

'No, he doesn't. It's perfect.'

Christo's voice behind them was as smooth and sleek against her skin as the silk lining of the dress.

Anna excused herself and slid from the room.

'You're lurking again.' Thea turned to face him. 'You know my thoughts on that.'

'That I'm untrustworthy?' His hands clenched and released, his fingers flexing restlessly.

Right now he most definitely did not look like a man who could be trusted. A shadow of stubble shaded his jaw. His hair looked as if he'd raked his hands through it one too many times. And all the while his hooded eyes devoured her in a dark, gleaming sweep from her neck to her feet and back again.

His charcoal three-piece suit was the only thing giving him any air of respectability. The rest of him looked irretrievably disreputable. A liquid heat bloomed deep and low inside.

'Yes. And I'm not wearing the dress.'

'Don't you like it?'

She ran her hands down the exquisite fabric. Too many emotions were coursing through her. 'No... Yes. It's beautiful.'

'Then why are you afraid?' The corners of his lips tipped in a knowing smile.

'I'm not afraid. I just want to wear the dress I picked for myself.'

He cocked his head to the side, looking at her as if she was some curious bejewelled butterfly. 'Let me guess. Plain? Black? One you can hide behind?'

'Stop saying those things!'

'Wear the gown I chose for you.'

He pointed to the mirror behind her. She turned.

'One that shows the magnificent woman you are.'

As she looked at her reflection Christo closed in behind her, his warmth solid at her back. The scent of him was intoxicating. Crisp. Wild. Pure male.

He reached out and placed his hands on the tops of her arms. She absorbed the quiet intimacy as his thumbs began to make slow circles. A shiver of pleasure at that beguiling touch began at the base of her neck and sparkled down her arms. There was a rightness in this picture. Something settling about them standing together like this.

'Your father and Demetri...'

He caught her reflected gaze, his hands continuing that gentle stroking. It was as if he was trying to delve into the soul of her.

'I'm sorry they have to be here. It can't be avoided.'

Thea looked to the floor. At the glittering perfection of her dress. Her twinkling shoes. He didn't need to see the vulnerability his decision had wrought in her.

'You won't tell me the reason?' she asked.

'I want more information before saying anything else.' Christo hesitated. 'You've been hurt enough by them. I won't add to your pain. If there was any other way...'

'You've said that before.' She shrugged. 'Yet here we are.'

He bent down, whispered in her ear. The breath caressing her throat.

'Courage, Thea.'

His voice rushed over her, hot and thick, with the same jolt as her morning coffee. Then he released her and stepped back. She mourned the loss of his hands on her skin.

'I'll see you downstairs in an hour.'

Thea's heart thundered as she walked down the curving staircase. She steadied herself on the balustrade. One moment she thought Christo understood her. The next...?

'Courage, Thea.'

What did he know of courage? Living his life of privilege. Not knowing fear. The dress didn't frighten her. Mere scraps of fabric couldn't hurt you. She knew where the real monsters hid—and tonight they'd be here, in this house.

She took a few breaths to calm herself and walked towards the ballroom. As she rounded a huge potted palm there Christo stood, towering in a perfectly tailored tuxedo, greeting his guests. The superfine wool moulded to the slim taper of his waist. His hands in the pockets of his trousers pulled them tight over his backside.

She stopped, hesitated, smoothed damp palms over the beaded fabric she wore. All the people terrified her. All this pretence. But she still had time; he hadn't seen her. She should change.

Instead she froze, her chest tightening. Where had all the air gone? Perspiration pricked the back of her neck as her hands curled into tight fists. She needed to walk backwards, walk *somewhere*, yet she couldn't take another step.

Thea knew the moment Christo realised she was there. His imposing shoulders straightened. His hands slid from his pockets and he turned.

'*Thea.*'

His low velvet voice penetrated the tension corseting her chest. He strode towards her, arm outstretched. She played the game. Placed her hand in his, felt it engulfed. He lifted it to his mouth, kissing the palm where seconds earlier her nails had bitten into her soft flesh. And in that act he stole her breath, caused a burn to heat her cheeks.

He looked down at her, his gaze all-seeing. And for a moment she lost herself in the calm ocean of his eyes. Her breathing eased. Her pounding heart steadied. Christo *did* understand. He understood too well.

'You look exquisite. I can see why red's your favourite colour.'

Her cheeks heated, no doubt flaming into the shade of her dress. 'Thank you. But it's too generous a gift.'

'It's nothing less than you deserve for all you've done. But sadly for now we must work. Perhaps later...?'

He raised an eyebrow and the corner of his mouth lifted in a lazy smile. A flush of warmth stole over her, Christo's invitation was clear. She could say yes and see what came of it.

Memories of that drizzly day in New York flooded into her consciousness. His hard, aroused body. Those deep, drugging kisses. A heavy pulse beat between her legs...

No, she had a part to play. That was all she could trust. Nothing more.

'You work too hard,' she said, focusing on what they had to do tonight.

Christo surveyed the crowd, as if he was making sure everyone appeared satisfied. But Thea could see what others didn't notice. The tightness around his eyes. The dull shadows underneath.

'My father would be proud.' He let out a slow breath, looked down at the floor. '*"Fun, fun, fun. That's all you want to have,"* he'd say to me. Other boys at school had holidays with their families. Hector sent me to work picking olives. I was nine.'

The thought of him being sent out to work so young was...shocking. She'd sometimes wondered about Christo as a small boy, what had made him the man he was. He always seemed so serious she wasn't sure he knew how to have fun. Perhaps with good reason.

She stared out at the throng of people. At least they seemed to be enjoying themselves as waiters threaded in and out with food and wine.

She said, 'That's—'

'Life. I learned long ago not to care.'

Thea wasn't so sure. His voice sounded flat and dead, as if he had to force himself not to dwell on it.

'Your father must be sorry he can't be here tonight,' she said.

Christo pinned her with his gaze, eyes hard and stormy. Time ticked for a few heartbeats, too much unsaid between them.

'I'm sure he is.'

'What about your mother?' Where had she been when her son was sent away to pick olives as a little boy? 'Surely she'll want to celebrate your success?'

'Ha! My mother?' He tensed, a muscle at the side of his jaw ticking. 'She's never cared. Always claimed I was an impossible child. Why would she feign interest now? The woman's as maternal as a cuckoo.'

How could his mother say such a thing? But his words explained too much. At least she'd had one parent love her unconditionally, and Alexis too. Didn't he have anyone?

'Christo…' Thea placed a hand on his arm, trying to offer some small comfort.

He shrugged her away. Snagged two glasses of champagne from a waiter and handed one chilled flute to her with a brittle smile.

'We should talk to some guests.'

His words spoke only of obligation. She didn't want to talk to the guests. She wanted to wrap her arms around the wounded boy she'd glimpsed in his tired eyes. The one driven by his father, abandoned by his mother. But he'd reject her sympathy, she was sure.

So instead she followed Christo into the crowd, the crush surrounding them. He patted people on the back, made small talk, smiled. But the smile didn't meet his eyes.

Thea smiled too, playing her part. No one commented on her tattoos, as she'd feared. A heady rush thrummed through her. She'd never hide them again. They weren't wounds. They spoke instead of her strength and survival.

As they turned to talk with yet another person who wanted a piece of her husband she saw them. In a corner. Talking to someone she didn't know. Her father and Demetri.

A tight knot of nausea gripped her belly. She stiffened.

Christo glanced in the direction she was looking. Then he frowned, turning to face her. She peered around him, unable to take her eyes from the two men.

Like a predator watching its prey, Demetri's cold stare met hers. Her heart raced, preparing for flight. She'd lived in a kind of peace without them in the same house. But even another continent was too close.

She wrapped her arms round her waist.

'I won't let them near you,' Christo said.

He slid his hand to the dip in her back and rested it there. The touch steadied her heart. His solid presence calmed the tightness in her stomach.

He looked over his shoulder, then back to her. 'Forget them. I have a small surprise for you.'

His voice was soft and low, as if soothing a terrified animal. He kept his body between her and the men of her family.

Thea realised he was shielding her from their gaze. She believed Christo now. As long as she was with him he'd protect her from Tito and Demetri. She shook off the sticky tendrils of fear. Those men would only win if she let them.

'My dress and jewels weren't enough of a surprise?'

His features darkened into that glorious brooding which made her heart skip a beat. With one hand he swept her hair back over her shoulder and toyed with an earring. When had his touching her become normal?

Thea allowed herself to melt into it, heat pooling in her belly. For a small while her world was reduced to Christo's gentle caress, encouraging the pretence that this could be something different. And for a brief, bright moment she wished it was real.

He shrugged. 'They're trinkets.'

She shook herself out of the dream, her stomach twisting, wondering how often he bestowed 'trinkets' upon other women.

What on earth was happening to her? She'd no right to these thoughts. Theirs was a convenient arrangement, and most women in this situation would be overjoyed by expensive gifts. She should learn to become one of them.

Thea gave him what she hoped was a gracious smile. 'How long are you going to keep me wondering?'

'Not long. I've invited Elena tonight.'

Her heart leapt with real joy. She hadn't spoken to her friend since her marriage—apart from a brief text from Elena saying her father was angry. Thea had a terrible feeling it had something to do with Elena's efforts to help *her*.

'Is she here yet?'

'Soon. But first come and meet the American ambassador and his wife. I think you'll like them.'

He swept her through the room, introducing her to more guests, never leaving her side. His hand was always at her back, its gentle pressure reassuring. His fingers stroked her body with the sway of her hips.

She became hyper-aware of every subtle touch. The way the luscious fabric of her gown fell against her as she moved. The caress of the satiny silk lining over her skin. Christo's choice. Christo's dress.

It was almost like his hands all over her. How much better would they feel than the silk that clothed her...? She craved it—craved his fingers exploring every curve, every secret place. The dark mystery that was Christo lit a burn deep inside her, flushing across her skin. Her nipples pebbled against the bodice of her dress, making every movement exquisite agony. She leaned into Christo's hard body, *all* of her attuned to him.

He tightened his arm around her. 'Elena's arrived,' he said, waking her from heated fantasies.

'Where?' Did he notice the huskiness of her voice? Christo gave no hint of it.

'In the corner—near the statue of Poseidon.'

She glimpsed her friend in a yellow dress and waved, trying to get her attention through the crush of guests.

'I'll take you to her. You've done enough smiling at strangers for me.'

'No. I'll go myself. You've too many people who need to congratulate you.'

Thea moved to leave Christo, slipping from his hold. The cool air where his hand had been felt like a loss.

He raised his eyebrows, stroking his hand down her arm till his fingers entwined in hers. He squeezed. 'You're sure?'

Thea looked up at him, her gaze snagging on the soft warmth in his green eyes, on his full lips which quirked at the corners.

The breath jagged in her throat. She needed to leave before she embarrassed herself. 'I'll be back shortly.'

'Take your time. You need some fun.' He kissed her hand in a perfect display of chivalry and let her go.

She hurried towards where she'd last seen her friend, excited to talk to her about how her life felt as if it were achieving some form of happiness, even in this arranged marriage.

'Thea.'

She froze. That familiar voice. Like being tossed into an icy river.

'You've been ignoring your father since you married. Talk to me a while.'

The old man himself stood there, arms out wide as if wanting to give her a hug. Smiling, but not with his eyes. They were a cold, muddy brown, fixed on her like a shark seeing prey in the water. She looked around furtively, but Christo was nowhere to be seen. The blood seeped to her toes and her vision blurred.

No. She was stronger than this. Her father was the weak one, bullying women. 'I've nothing to say to you.'

'Young love! You've forgotten your family.' He laughed.

The mirthless sound ran like frigid water through her veins. 'Family? I've no family here.'

Tito's eyes narrowed. There was nothing but disdain on his face now. 'What would your husband have to say to that?'

Thea gritted her teeth. 'He's no part of this conversation.

You sold me off for your own interests and then broke your promise to me about Alexis!'

To anyone watching it would look as though father and daughter were having a close conversation. But a war was being waged here. One she wouldn't lose.

'Your bastard half-brother will be interested to know how you're playing with his future.' Her father continued to give her that dead smile. 'I gave you clear instructions. Where's the information I want?'

She'd never even considered giving her father any information about Christo's company, and yet here was more confirmation that Alexis had paid the price for her decisions. The ache of it cut deep inside.

'Get the information yourself! You don't own me now. You passed that privilege on to Christo and he won't help you.'

Her father moved in close, looming over her. She wavered, the sick feeling at his proximity clawing at her throat. But she wouldn't cower, and she wouldn't hide. Not anymore.

'I'm sure you could convince him to do anything you wanted.' Her father's hard mouth turned up in a sneer, as if he'd stepped in something bad. 'Using your charms, your lies. It's in your breeding, with that mother of yours.'

She took a step back, the roil of her anger burning fierce. How dared he mention Maria, when he'd tried to obliterate her memory for so many years?

'Demetri has the same mother. Or have your forgotten that convenient fact? Watch your back, Father.'

'I can ruin Christo and you with him. Don't think it's beneath me.'

She folded her arms and narrowed her eyes. 'I don't think anything's beneath you. You'd eat from the gutter if it advantaged you.'

'Careful, Thea. You want money and privilege? I'll take all of this away if you don't do what I ask.'

She laughed. The deluded man thought he had the power of God. 'How can you take it? You'd never have sold me off to anyone who wasn't richer than Croesus.'

'Christo hasn't told you anything?'

Tito's eyes widened, and his smile morphed into one of pure evil. What was he planning?

A terrible chill slid through her. 'I don't under—'

Her father looked over her shoulder. 'Here's your brother to talk some sense into you.'

A shadow loomed behind her. Her father's words could slice like a dagger, but Demetri inflicted real pain. From pulling her hair as a child, he had progressed, unchecked by a father who didn't care about the little girl who was a constant reminder of the wife who'd left him.

Demetri's hand clamped tight on her arm. 'Sense? She's a disgrace.'

'Don't touch me!'

But no one would notice. She was on her own. These men had perfected sleight of hand, could hurt in ways which would never be seen.

'Have you looked at her back, Father? She's displaying a monstrosity.' Demetri leaned down to hiss in her ear. 'I suspected you were cheap, but you've outdone yourself.'

He pulled her around slyly, so no one would notice. He was clever that way. Her arm burned in his tight grip. But she wouldn't let him see her fear. She never had.

'How could your husband allow you to deface yourself?' her father spat.

She wrenched her arm from Demetri's crushing fingers. He'd never touch her again—not if she could help it. Thea drew herself up to face them, proudly displaying her tattoos—the symbols of her ultimate freedom. Even Christo had recognised that.

Christo.

He was cutting through the crowd. Purpose etched on his face. Eyes hard. Mouth a thin, cruel line. Looking as if he was ready to draw blood as his gaze slid from her father to Demetri. Blind fury from this man who always seemed implacable.

Her heart beat a little faster as he shouldered through his guests.

'You can ask me yourself.'

Christo's eyes were focused on her. She forgot everything, lost in his hot green gaze. Forgot the hatred tightening in her belly, the burning of her arm where Demetri's fingers had been.

Her father watched him, took a step back and plastered on his usual fake smile. 'An excellent party, Christo. It does Atlas Shipping's history great justice.'

Tito Lambros played the charming man well. She knew better. He might sound warm and interested. She could feel the strike of cold steel underneath.

Christo pushed between her and Demetri, towering over the men in her family.

'Are you troubling Thea?'

No niceties from her husband. His voice was stark and brutal. He wrapped his arm around her waist, drawing her close.

'Someone needs to keep her under control,' said Demetri.

Christo turned to her brother and pinned him with a withering look. 'What are you afraid of, Demetri? That if you let Thea be herself she'll outwit you? I'm sorry to say she already has.'

'She's making a mockery of us—displaying herself in that dress,' her father drawled, looking her up and down as if she was tainted.

'The only thing I see is an exquisite woman wearing the gift I gave her.' Christo's hand squeezed her hip. 'If you and your son don't appreciate that, you can leave our home.'

Her father held up his hands as if in surrender. Thea knew too well it was only for show.

'A piece of advice, Christo, from an older man who's

been married to a younger woman. It's easy to be blinded by beauty. Let your wife rule your home at your peril. Take your father—'

'I'll only take advice on marriage from a person who's had a successful one.'

Thea had never really taken notice of how her father, brother and Christo were together. Now she saw. Their dislike was palpable, and the air vibrated with mutual loathing.

'Then we'll leave you both to your obvious happiness.' Her father turned to her and fixed her with his reptilian gaze. 'Remember what I said. We'll have lunch. It's been too long since we've seen you.'

She shivered. The thought of sitting down to a meal with her father was about as welcome as the thought of being thrown into a tank of piranha fish.

'Yes,' said Demetri, looking at them both with contempt. 'Tonight isn't the time. It's all about celebrating your husband's exploits.'

As Demetri moved to go Christo gripped his arm, his tanned knuckles blanching as he did so. The two men stood there, glaring at each other. Demetri's gaze was tinged with fear; Christo's brimmed with pure hatred.

His lips contorted in a false smile, vicious and predatory. 'Touch Thea again and I will make you bleed.'

She gasped. The threat so bold, the violence underlying it so blatant.

Demetri said nothing. He nodded his head and wrenched his arm away, scuttling into the crowd.

Thea wilted. The only thing holding her upright was Christo's strong arm around her waist.

Dipping his head, he murmured, 'We need some time. Come with me.'

He steered her through the crowd to a quiet corner behind some freshly installed midnight-blue velvet curtains. Her whole body shook. Christo wrapped his arms around her. Drew her close. He'd said he'd protect her, and he had. That meant more to her than she could ever have imagined.

She rested her head on his chest, relishing his warmth. He stroked her back as her shivering subsided, whispering gentle words.

'I should never have left you alone... I didn't believe they'd be brazen enough... Not in our home...'

Everyone would think they were having a touching moment. No one would realise he was stitching her back together. Soothing her with his quiet strength. The solid beat of his heart.

'I'm fine now,' she said, pulling away. 'I need to go and find Elena. You invited her here for me.'

Christo cupped her jaw, looked into her eyes. She hated that he could see everything—especially her weakness.

'Are you sure? You don't have to stay any longer. I can say you were tired.'

She shook her head. 'Now you've put my father and Demetri in their place it'll be okay.'

Or would it? Considering what her father had said, the threats he'd made? She needed to warn Christo.

'My father said he could ruin you. Take everything away. Is that true?'

A flash of red heightened his cheeks and Christo dropped his head, a frown marring his perfect features. He shoved his hands in the pockets of his trousers. 'I should have told you.'

'About what?'

His shoulders rose and fell with a slow breath. 'Atlas owes money to your father's bank. Hector let the payments fall behind. Our marriage prevented your father calling in the debt.'

A terrible chill ran through her. Her father's ruthlessness in business was renowned. He would have used the situation to his every advantage. Christo had said in the beginning that he needed her. She hadn't realised how badly.

'How did this happen?'

Christo's jaw clenched hard. The party carried on around them. Champagne flowed. Such a celebration. And yet there was nothing to celebrate at all.

'My father should have learned. But, no. On a quest for the love of a woman he looked in the wrong place. *Again.*'

'Where was your mother?'

'Long gone. With a flamenco dancer, I believe.' He gave a mirthless laugh. 'My birth was a cunningly laid trap to secure my father's fortune, since he wouldn't have any *bastardos* walking the streets. They married, I was born, it ended—although they never divorced. She came back occasionally, when his purse strings were pulled too tight. He adored her, despite everything. I suspect he still does. But love makes fools of men.'

Thea knew now why Christo didn't believe in love. What kind of example had either of them been set? Both had been trapped in broken, hateful families.

'I'm sorry.'

Christo shook his head, his mouth twisted in a sneer of disgust. 'Hector always sought replacements to fill the hole my mother left. It was as if his only son didn't matter. He became involved with an antiquities dealer. Beautiful, exotic. He threw away a fortune on priceless treasures for her. The business suffered as my father ignored it. That's why he had to go begging to your father—to hide his humiliation. I found out too late.'

He looked around the room, hard lines of rage bracketing his mouth. 'Then I discovered some of the objects he'd purchased had been illegally obtained. I suspect from shipments of looted items. That alone could have ruined us. I'd like to believe my father didn't know, but the fool would have done anything for the alluring Miss Carvallo.'

Thea's heart rate spiked. She knew that name. 'Ramona Carvallo?'

Christo's eyes narrowed. 'Yes.'

'I think I've met her—at my father's home.'

He reached up his hand, sliding it through her hair to cup the back of her neck. His thumb traced a gentle line along her jaw, forcing her to look at him. Deep into the green storm of his eyes. He moved his head towards her, leaned down, his lips to her ear. And Thea's eyes drifted shut at the light brush of his warm breath on her skin.

'Look over my shoulder at the woman in the corner of the room. Purple dress. Do you recognise her?'

Thea didn't want to wake from this dream where they meant something to each other. She relished the intimacy even if its purpose was serious. Still, she did as he asked.

When her eyes focused, she saw her. 'Ramona Carvallo,' she whispered.

Christo's lips began drifting a fiery path down her neck. She sighed and melted into the heat of him. What they were doing might be hiding the true purpose of this conversation, but she craved every inch of his body melded against hers.

'Why invite her here?' she asked. Having this woman in his home might only inflame the very scandal he was trying to avoid.

Christo pulled back, his pupils dark, his breathing heavy. Matching hers. She regretted the broken intimacy.

'Raul's organising security,' he said. 'His operatives are in the crowd...watching.'

'What for?'

'Your father used information about the smuggled objects as leverage against my father—the risk of disgrace, jail... I wondered how your father had found out about them. I suspect Tito and Ramona were working together. I want to see if your father reacts to her. People make mistakes. Especially arrogant, entitled people. I'm relying on it happening here.'

'And if it doesn't?'

'Then it won't change anything you and I have agreed.'

That was the least of her worries. She realised now the

reason why he'd been working those long hours. The parties, the meetings…what he'd required of her. He wasn't only inheriting the company. He was saving it.

'I also hope to find out whether your father purchased anything questionable.'

'So you can use it against him like he did to Hector?'

'To stop him stealing Atlas? Yes.'

Could her father have bought illegal objects to add to his collection? Whilst she wasn't aware he'd ever actually broken the law, she wouldn't put it past him. He believed himself to be above everyone else. And after all he'd done to her she'd give anything to stop her father taking what wasn't his.

'He owns a vast collection of old things,' she said.

Heat flared in Christo's eyes. She wished it was for her, but she knew it was for the hope he'd described. Still, there was more she needed to tell him. The information her father had requested took on more significance now.

'There's something else,' she said. 'He demanded I get him information about Atlas. Shipping details. Ports of docking and unloading. Names of the captains on each vessel's journey.'

'Interesting…' Christo said.

It was. Most of those details were publicly available. She'd only investigated out of curiosity. Her father didn't need her to find out anything. A shipping broker could have done the job as easily.

'And did you give your father the information?'

Christo's voice was cool, his face impassive. He didn't trust her, even after what she'd divulged. A pang of hurt scored her insides.

'Never! That's why they said Alexis stole money. To ensure my compliance.' Her voice cracked.

Christo wrapped his arms around her again, drawing her tight to him. 'Thea. I'm sorry. Raul will find him.'

Unless her father got to Alexis first.

She slumped into Christo, exhaustion washing over her.

The night was going to be long, and all she wanted was to stay like this for ever. In Christo's arms. Where, for once, everything felt natural and right. But there was no 'for ever' for them—only now. And if that was all she had she'd take it. Because this wasn't Christo's fault—or hers. They were both pawns in a rich man's game.

And as she nestled into Christo's chest, soaking up the heat into her frozen heart, she knew. The blackmail… This marriage… It wasn't about a debt. Her father wanted Christo's ships.

CHAPTER TEN

HE'D FAILED. NOT on all measures tonight. But on the most important his failure had been acute—because he'd failed Thea.

Christo dropped his head, stared at the floor. A piece of lint was attached to his shoe. He kicked off the polished black leather. Tore at his bow tie and tossed it on the couch. The taint of bile rose in his throat.

His presumptions tonight disgusted him. What had he been thinking? He'd dared Thea to wear that dress. To show everyone the woman he saw each day. Show her magnificence. Show she was a force of nature, alive and powerful in a flash of arterial red.

She'd cut every man off at the knees when she'd walked into the room. His baser parts had brimmed with pride at having her by his side as she'd threaded her arm through his. Yet he'd brought the enemy into his home. Drawn her father and brother to her and hadn't been there to stop them.

It haunted him. Her standing there, surrounded. Demetri clasping her arm in that brutal grip. Volcanic heat clawed his gut. He flexed his fingers. How dared *anyone* lay their hands on her? After all she'd confessed, the least she was due was his protection and he couldn't even give her that properly.

He unbuttoned his shirt. Shrugged it off. Poured a cognac. He'd let another burn, that of the amber liquid, scorch away the guilt.

The celebrations had been a success. He'd done his duty by Atlas. Raul could assess the rest. Demetri and Tito's arrogance had overcome their good sense. It showed they could be caught out if watched closely enough.

He gulped from the glass, downing the contents in one mouthful. He'd try to sleep—a futile activity since Thea had entered his house. He'd wake to visions of smooth skin and breathless sighs as he immersed himself in a soft, warm body. The dreams were fevered, formless things, but he knew who he was with. Who shared with him the pleasure they unleashed. Thea. Always Thea.

He had no right to her. But the feel of her supple body in his arms tonight, her head on his chest as she melted into him...

Even as he'd been soothing her he'd been craving her. The only one he desired. Of all the women who'd sought him out over the years, he coveted the one who didn't want him. The relentless hunger of it ached inside him.

You're married to her.

No! He had to shut out that voice, whispering the impossible. Her trust had been betrayed by too many. He still had some honour left. A thin shred, which frayed a little more every time she came near, but he'd protect it. Try to stitch it up with more resolve than he'd ever shown in the past when he'd seen something he wanted to reach out and take.

She'd leave this marriage untouched. This constant ache was his penance for every selfish deed of his past. He *would* be better. For her.

A tentative knock sounded at the door. It opened a crack and the soft music of her voice filled the space. 'I want to thank you.'

His heart plummeted as Thea drifted into the room, still dressed in the glittering gown he'd chosen. The soft lace accentuated her hypnotic curves. His goddess. A dream that couldn't be. Thea had loaned him her life just for a short while. She wasn't his to keep.

Yet seductive whispers of *Kiss her...* filled his head. He shut them down.

'You've nothing to thank me for.' The words were ground out like broken glass, cutting with each utterance. He did want her thanks. He wanted it all.

'You stood up for me.'

Her eyes gleamed bright in the soft lamplight. His desire to comfort her overwhelmed him. To wrap her up tight and stroke away her pain. All dangerous ideas designed to get her into his arms again.

'It was no more than anyone would have done,' he said.

She shook her head. 'You know that's not true.'

He noticed the marks on her skin from Demetri's rough fingers. She'd bruise. Cold, dark certainty chilled through his veins. He'd break the man who had done that to her.

He took a step forward. Stopped. 'Your arm—'

She shrugged it off. 'I've had worse.'

Her acceptance crushed him. The things she'd endured... 'You're safe now. Your father and brother will *never* hurt you again.'

She looked up at him with warm amber eyes. The fire from them beat any drink in a glass.

'I know.'

She'd invaded his senses. He wanted to immerse himself in her scent of sweet spice. *Touch her...* Touch those red marks on her arm.

He reached out and stroked them. Her skin was smooth silk under his fingertips. Her pupils dilated and she blinked, long and slow. Her lashes feathered her cheek. A lick of heat curled deep inside him and clenched tight.

'I trust you, Christo.'

Her voice brushed feather-soft against his skin. *Take her...* He'd sweep her into his arms. Ravish her plush scarlet lips. Replace pain with gasping pleasure.

Christo glimpsed her reflection in the mirror behind them. That sinuous flock of birds soared across her spine. He would never forget that one of those birds had been tattooed there for him. He was required to atone for it.

'You shouldn't,' he said, though still every part of him yearned to protect her. For ever.

He removed his hand from the warmth of her and

clenched his fists by his sides. Relegated himself to a life
of cold. 'I do what advantages me and no one else.'

Was she cold too? Goose bumps bloomed on her arms.
Her lips parted. Her eyes were alight, blazing and fierce.
The silence stretched the space between them till every
part of him screamed to fill it. Her thoughts were so loud
he could almost hear them.

I see through you.

To the child he'd once been. Unloved. Unlovable.

She cocked her head. 'Who's the liar now?'

Aching hunger gripped his gut. He couldn't give her
what she deserved. *Love.* It wasn't an emotion he felt and
she needed someone to cherish her. She contained too much
life and passion to be kept by a man like him.

Yet how he longed to release it all. To scorch himself
clean. He abhorred any man who'd seen her before. He
wanted to be her past, present and future. It was a cruel,
impossible desire.

She had her past. He'd seen snatches of it from the file
Raul had created. Grainy pictures and the hidden treasure
she'd permitted him to glimpse. Though no matter how
deeply he delved he'd never unwrap all of her, wound in
mystery as she was.

'It's a warning. One you should heed.'

He should send her away, safe to her room. Drink some
more and drown out the dreams which lured him to purgatory each night.

'Goodnight, Thea.'

He was close to her now. How they'd moved together he
couldn't tell. Were they his steps or hers?

She reached up, hesitated. Her slender hand hovered
in the space between them. Then her eyes dropped to his
mouth and she touched him. A tentative brush on his jaw.
The burn of anticipation for things he'd never take roared
through him. If he stood there, unmoving, she'd stop. He'd
allow her this faltering exploration. Succumb to weakness

and accept her soft caresses. It was all he could ever allow himself.

She traced his bottom lip, and the sting of pleasure rippled through him as her searching fingers trapped his gusting breaths. Her gaze followed everywhere she touched. Like his throat, where she hesitated on the pulse of his heart slamming into his ribs. Her lips tilted. Then cool fingers on heated flesh traced the muscles of his chest, as if the wonders of the universe were written in Braille on his skin. The merest brush over his nipple made his breath hitch.

His eyes drifted shut, trying to lock her out. Still her hand explored every ridge of his abdomen, till he was on fire. An inferno threatened to devour him.

He snapped his hand over hers. 'Stop.'

Every part of him screamed for her to go on. He'd never craved anything more. Atlas Shipping? He'd sign it all away for her fingers to continue their cartography of his body. But she wasn't his. He wouldn't take her.

He opened his eyes. Hers were heavy-lidded, with a sultry golden glow. She stepped back, slid her hand from under his. Broke their touch. The loss of her was immediate and brutal. But a quiet, knowing smile tilted the corners of her mouth.

Thea reached around and drew down the tiny zipper at the back of her dress. Christo watched the mirror behind her, as if in slow motion. Each notch of the zip punched another hit of lust into his gut. She tugged at the bow holding the halter neck and shrugged the dress free. Red lace slithered over her body, caressing each curve as it fell. She stood there. Bare except for the glittering heels and the tiny scrap of a G-string covering the apex of her thighs. The dress swirled at her feet, the colour of blood.

That should be his blood on the floor. His sacrifice to this goddess, all honeyed skin and slender waist and perfect breasts, her nipples taut and ripe. Ready for him.

'Thea…' His voice rasped, unrecognisable. A plea? A

prayer of thanks? He couldn't tell. He wanted all she was offering. Wanted to consume her. But he'd leave nothing behind if he had his way.

'Please, Christo…'

He shook his head, trembling with the effort of ignoring the desire raging through him. 'Not for me.'

'You're worth it.'

He wasn't. But those words… They broke him.

He strode forward. Wrapped his arms around her and grasped the smooth, warm flesh under his hands. Her skin was warm satin against his palms. She melted into him. Sighed as he took her lips with his. His tongue plundered her luscious mouth. She was tentative at first, before softening into the rhythm, willing and hungry.

She lifted her hands to his hair and he shivered at the scrape of her fingernails against his scalp. He slipped his hands to her buttocks, round and bare, holding her against his hard, aching body.

She ground against him, mewling and desperate. If he didn't get her to the bed soon they'd both finish here. He hooked his fingers into her flimsy underwear, slid it past her hips and let it fall to the floor. He battled with the fly of his trousers and cast them aside with his briefs. Thank God he was only half dressed, so he wouldn't have to waste more time. He was a wreck of desire.

He swept Thea into his arms and lowered her onto the bed. She scrambled back against the pillows, her body splayed out like an offering. Waiting. He slid a hand along the smooth swell of her calf. She dropped her head back and moaned. He eased off one stiletto, and then the other, all the while indulging in a visual feast of her golden skin and luxurious curves. Glowing, wanton and perfect.

'I'm coming for you, Thea.'

She shivered as he crawled over the top of her, his vision fogged by the red roar of arousal. Her dusky pink nipples peaked in hard points. He bent down and lavished one with the attention of his tongue. Her low cries of pleasure pierced the room. She smelled of spices and musk. Exotic. Delectable. Driving him on. Driving him to madness.

He was so hard he'd shatter before long. And Thea's body trembled at each touch. He needed her warm softness to envelop him. His mouth watered at the thought of the night ahead. Devouring her body. Pleasuring her till dawn. Taking the pleasure he'd denied himself. Now she was *his*.

He lay next to her, sliding his hand down her stomach, easing his fingers into the dark triangle of hair at the apex of her thighs, exploring the hot, plush folds of her. She arched into him as he stroked her there. He wanted to watch her fall apart, but that would be the end of him. She was everything. Too much. Like a dream he'd awoken into.

He rolled away. Grappled with protection. If he let her touch him he'd explode. He moved over her again. Settled between trembling thighs which had fallen open for him. He was beyond sanity, almost beyond all control. And then that thinnest of threads snapped. She was here. She was ready. *Thea.*

In one fluid movement he thrust hard and took what was his. And as he buried himself in the heart of her body he realised he'd made a terrible mistake.

Too fast. Too much. Too *everything.* The fire consumed her, deep inside. And Christo above her. Still, silent apart from his ragged breaths. She was trying not to breathe. Not to move. If she didn't, it might not hurt.

Was it meant to be like this? She'd had orgasms before, on her own. They were fun, and she'd assumed with someone else it would be even better.

But tonight? All the pleasure, and then…

She stiffened.

Christo dropped his forehead to hers. His strong, muscular arms bracketed the sides of her head, his heavy weight pressing her down.

'You should have told me.'

His voice was gentle. Kind. Her humiliation, complete.

'It didn't seem important.'

Virginity wasn't, was it? An outdated notion, she'd always thought. Till now.

His muscles quivered. Was it hard for him to hold himself like that? She wasn't sure. He'd been so hungry. Passionate. *Aroused.* Though she hadn't really anything to go by, when he'd said he was coming for her she'd almost burst into flames. And then as he'd crawled towards her, wild and wanting...

The size of him. For a moment passion had fled and fear had invaded, leaching in like poison. Then he'd plunged into her, and now they were here.

'It's everything, Thea.'

His breath brushed her cheek. He tried to move—a slight shift as if to gently withdraw. Her hands that had been bunching the sheets in tight fingers now grabbed his hips to still him.

'No. It's done.'

She wanted him, craved to give him all of herself. How could this have gone so wrong?

'That doesn't give me much comfort.'

His laugh was mirthless. Pained. Though her own pain seemed to be dulling. Maybe she was getting used to him. The burn felt different now—less fire more insistence. A sensation she couldn't place.

She moved her hands to his arms and stroked his taut biceps. Her each inhalation was a mere sip of air. What had started out as a grand seduction, had turned into a disaster.

Christo leaned down and brushed his lips over hers. 'You said you trusted me. Do you still trust me, Thea?'

She nodded. Because she did. Implicitly. She knew he'd never intended what had happened tonight.

'You need to breathe,' he said. 'Slowly.'

She looked into his eyes, green pools of swirling emotion.

'Relax. I know what I'm doing.'

She breathed and he withdrew. The relief was exquisite, but a terrible feeling of loss remained. She didn't understand it at all.

He cradled her in his arms. 'I've disappointed you,' she said, her voice cracking.

'No.' He held her close against his chest. All the while running his hand over her quaking body. 'You've honoured me.'

He kissed the side of her neck, feather-light. Goose bumps flowered from every touch of his lips, shivering over her. He continued to stroke her everywhere his gentle fingers could reach. Smoothing out the tense muscles till she relaxed.

He whispered into her ear. 'In this bed there's only pleasure. I promise.' Heat flashed over her, a new burn replacing the old. That confusing ache between her legs remained. Grew. She wanted him again—but how could that be?

He kissed her. His lips soft and gentle. Exploring slowly, waiting for her. She kissed him back. Every sweep of his tongue encouraged her to drown in the pleasure of his mouth. His hands drifted over her skin, stroking her nipples with the pad of his thumb till they were tight and all too sensitive. She wanted his tongue on them again. That sharp spike of pleasure spearing straight to her core.

As if reading her mind, he took her left nipple into his mouth, lavishing it with attention as his hand slipped between her legs.

Her stomach clenched with fear, but he soothed it away with his gentle insistent touch, coaxing her. The fire took hold, deep and low. He stroked, finding the perfect spot. There. *There.* The spark arced between her nipple and the juncture of her thighs. Pleasure. Pain. Beyond comprehension.

He slid one finger deep inside. Withdrew it. Then two. She gasped. The air was thick and hard to breathe. He kept moving, in a slow, hypnotic rhythm. Oh, this… *This* was how it was meant to be. All-consuming.

The rhythm inside her was mirrored by his tongue at her nipple. He moved his thumb to the sensitive nerves between her legs. A light circling and the heat bloomed in a rush from her centre, roaring outwards. There was nothing but the feel of him. Lips, tongue, fingers. The wet slickness of her.

She needed him inside her again. Was desperate for him to fill her. He didn't, just continued the relentless rhythm.

'*Christo…*'

His name undid her. She screamed it to the room, and then she flew. Gripped him hard as wave after wave of perfection flooded over her. Her mind soared and her body followed. Convulsing. Gasping. Out of control. True freedom.

The spasms subsided. He withdrew his hand. Every part of her was shimmering with pleasure as he lay over her again and eased into her body. Gently. With reverence. She sighed. There was no pain. Only relief.

She placed her hands on his buttocks. Gripped him as the muscles tensed with each thrust. She understood desire now. Understood why it could drive a person mad.

Christo. Inside her. Close. Perfect. Elemental.

The pressure built again as she rode with him, two bodies in unison. Each thrust plunged him deeper and deeper into the soul of her. Into the sticky, sweet mess of it. And this time it was less sharp, but no less devastating. A long, blissful ache that built and built till her control shattered right along with his.

He moaned her name. Pained? Pleasured? She wasn't sure. And then she let herself be swept away on the tide of it again.

CHAPTER ELEVEN

CHRISTO SLID INTO consciousness as the hazy veil of slumber lifted, to find his body curled around a luscious female form. The sun had barely begun to rise. Faint birdsong twittered in the garden. The room lay dusky and still, apart from her steady breaths.

Thea...

He buried his face in the warm silk of her hair. The honey-eyed smell of her wrapped seductively around him. Every part of him ached to ease into her warm, soft body again.

He wouldn't wake her. But the need clutched at his throat and threatened to cut off his breath. He had no rights here. He shouldn't have touched her. Even worse, he'd taken her virginity. The guilt of it scraped inside him.

He'd been fooled by those photographs in Raul's dossier. She'd been right from the beginning. He was no better than the rest of them. He'd seen only what he'd wanted to and taken selfishly. No matter how much she claimed to desire him, he'd used her in the crudest fashion.

It made him sick to his gut. Even though his body screamed for her, rigid with desire.

They were married. He could take her and what would it matter?

But it did. He'd said he'd protect her. From her father and brother, sure. But from himself too. He was just another man wanting to use her for his own aims. No matter how he tried to dress it up in some cloak of honour.

He dragged his reluctant body away from hers, putting some space between them. She stirred, sighed and sank back into the pillows. He watched her sleep. Stared at the dip and curve of her waist. The flare of her hip. Her hair like spilled coffee on the pillow.

Then there were the tattoos. When he'd first seen them, in his arrogance he'd thought they marred her. Not now. He reached out, his hand tracing the serpentine flock that swooped across her spine, each one a tribute to her strength in the face of deprivation.

He stroked his finger across the last bird. *His*. Acid burned his throat. His mark on her. He could never forget.

Thea stretched, lean limbs tightening. Then she turned, her eyes heavy with sleep. A soft smile played on her plush, plum-coloured mouth. She looked wanton. Well kissed.

He bunched his hands by his sides, but there was no hiding the arousal which had plagued him since he'd woken. Her eyes flicked to it, and back to him. She licked her lips. He had to do something—because he wasn't going to take any more from her. Even if she thought she wanted to give it freely.

'When are you going to add another bird?' His voice was rough with lust. He cleared his throat.

Her brows knitted. Confusion flitted over her face. 'Why would I do that?'

'I hurt you.'

The simple truth. One she couldn't deny.

Thea put her hand to his cheek. It rested there. Soft and cool against his burning skin.

'You gave me wings.'

She'd misunderstood him. He'd taken from her. Taken something he'd had no right to.

'You were in pain.'

Her thumb stroked gently back and forth across his cheek. Her eyes locked onto his, dark and serious.

'A few nerves. It was nothing.'

He took her hand in his and squeezed. 'I've marked you. Worse than your brother. Worse than your father.'

She sat up, filling his vision with her unique glow. Her hair tumbled over her shoulders to skim her rosy pink nipples. He wanted to drag her down, let her light spill into him. Flood the dark corners of his soul.

'No, Christo.' Her eyes were wide with horror. 'Never compare yourself to them. It was perfect.'

He should turn away, but the view of her luscious body filled him. His gaze raked over her. She looked down at him, grasped the sheet in front of her and dragged it to her chest. Her cheeks flushed. That picture of innocence made her look even more beautiful, and it was a reminder.

'Your virginity isn't something you should have given me. Anyone else—'

'I've never met anyone I thought worthy.'

Her words sliced through him. Her eyes were wide and soulful. They tore at his heart.

'You're worthy of me,' she whispered.

How could he tell her he was not that person?

He wasn't good enough. Not even his parents wanted him. But he craved to be a better man—one who'd never hurt her.

That bereft, lost look in her eyes haunted him. Christo hauled her close and she fell into his arms. He threaded his hands through her hair, dropping his lips to hers. He lost himself in her sweet intoxication. He couldn't give her much, but he could give her this.

He rolled away from her and she whimpered in protest, smiling as he returned, sheathed, protected and ready. He eased her leg over his hip, bringing her close. She arched towards him. He was hard. Desperate to be inside her. Each breathy sigh pleaded with him to thrust into her body. But he held back. There'd be no clumsy attempt this morning. He wanted it slow and aching. So he could watch her tremble and fall apart as he filled her with consuming pleasure.

He reached his hands around to her perfect buttocks, drawing her close. She sighed as her eyes drifted shut. He slid his hands between her legs, teasing between her thighs till she begged—'Please...'—and he slid one finger inside. Another circled her clitoris till she trembled in his arms.

She lifted her head and looked at him. Eyes glassy,

breaths short and panting. He angled his hips towards her and entered her with a slow slide that almost undid him. She moaned—a deep, satisfying thing that punched low and hard. He kept his hand between them, teasing as he pulled her leg higher over his hip and maintained the aching rhythm between her thighs.

He looked into her glazed, desire-drugged face. He wanted her. More than life. The curl of need at his every move into her body twisted tight and threatened to snap him. He was close. So close. But he'd ensure her pleasure first. Her nipples had tightened and her breathing had become ragged. Every part of her was taut, as if she were hanging by a gossamer thread. Like she needed permission to let go.

'Come for me, Thea.'

A final thrust and she gasped, as if starved for air. He lost all restraint as Thea threw her head back and sobbed out his name like some prayer to the heavens. Then the brittle seam holding him together ripped wide and he tore apart with her.

They lay for a while, his forehead against hers. Their panting breaths filled the room. Then he scooped her into his arms, showering her with soft kisses. He made a silent promise. He'd keep Thea safe for as long as he had her.

She raised her head. Her eyes were unfocused, her mouth red and soft.

'Christo…?'

She wanted answers he couldn't give.

He stroked a tendril of damp hair from her cheek. The birds outside sang louder now, but the dawn hadn't broken fully. They had a few more hours to rest. A few more hours and then she'd leave his bed and he must never do this again. How could he, when he had nothing to offer her? Until then he had time to revel in her touch.

The grief of how little was left stabbed at the heart of him. He cradled her to his chest. 'Sleep, *koukla mou*.' He closed his eyes as she softened in his arms.

CHAPTER TWELVE

'I'LL BE GONE a week—perhaps more.'

And so he'd left her. Alone.

Thea had offered to travel with him, but Christo had refused. For the few days before he'd left there'd been no breakfasts together. Even at night he'd turned her away. Said there was no longer any need for the charade, that everyone accepted their marriage as a proper one.

The rejection twisted her inside, but it didn't quell her desire. Nothing doused the fever he'd awakened. She dreamed of hard, entwined bodies, only to wake exhausted. Filled her days with thoughts only of him.

What had he done to her? This was like some illness. She couldn't escape the memory of pleasure, of the fire he'd lit. It consumed her.

Thea wanted more. Much more. She understood their arrangement, but surely both of them could be adults and enjoy the time they had together?

It will burn you to ashes.

She didn't care. The only thing that would soothe her was Christo. His body was like cool water on the flames.

'When are you going to add another bird?'

Such a strange thing to say. Surely he couldn't believe he'd hurt her after she'd cried out his name and lain sated in his arms? But he did—she was convinced of it. The way he'd avoided her before he left... Treated her with such care and reverence... Arranged full use of his yacht, warning the staff on his island that she may come...

But all she wanted to do was follow him around the world. Surprise him with some of the more exotic lingerie she still hadn't worn.

He wouldn't be able to resist. Because she had seen the

fire in him too. The hazel eyes which darkened to jade whenever she was near. The kiss goodbye that had pretended to be a chaste brush on the cheek but had ended in his low groan. Still he had denied himself.

And yet she recognised that Christo was gripped by some strange sense of honour. She had to prove to him that she understood.

Sure, Christo had promised he would soon have enough information about her father's illegal activities. Inviting him and her brother to the party had been a success. But she needed to repay Christo for the care he'd shown her, no matter what he said.

Which was why she was taking a risk.

She'd come up with a plan to go to her former home and look for more proof of her father's link with Ramona Carvallo. The problem was, she didn't know what to look for. All she could be certain of was that the house held answers, somewhere.

A dark shiver ran through her at the thought of crossing that threshold again, but she ignored it. She had to be strong for Christo. It was the only way.

Thea walked to the front of the house, where Sergei waited with the car. She slid into the back seat, her heart pounding in a sickening rhythm.

There was no need for fear. Her father wouldn't be there—she'd checked. And the staff still had some loyalty to her. She'd been the one to buy them Christmas gifts and to care when their children were ill. In turn they'd cared for her as her father never had. Tito Lambros might pay them, but they didn't like him.

Still, she needed a ruse in case he returned unexpectedly. It was a slim prospect, but she wanted to protect the people who'd been her only real family in that house as much as she protected herself. Everyone would believe her if she said she was looking for the necklace her mother had given her. She unclasped it from around her neck and dropped it into the pocket of her handbag.

The drive wasn't a long one, but as Sergei pulled up at the golden gates and high white walls she was reminded how much she loathed the crass opulence of the place.

'I'll get out here. Wait for me around the corner in the side street. You'll see a small wooden door.'

Sergei narrowed his eyes. 'Are you sure, Mrs Callas?'

No, she wasn't sure about this. The old, dark fears had begun to cloud her vision, chatter in her head. But she looked Sergei straight in the eye.

'Yes. I won't be long.'

She got out of the car. The heat of the day assaulted her, threatening to choke the air from her lungs. Thea pressed the buzzer and the gate opened. She stopped, took a deep breath and walked through, up the long, sloping drive. Each footfall took her closer to the house which held all her grief and tears.

When her mother had left, her world ended. Her father knew judges, lawyers. He'd fought to keep Thea not because he loved her, but because he'd wanted revenge. And still Maria had made her way back. Through the side door where Sergei now waited. Secreted in the servants' quarters so they could snatch a few minutes of happiness before she had to leave again.

Demetri had been lost even then. And one day her mother had become lost to her as well.

She forced away the memories as she made her way to the massive doors of the house. They cracked open as she arrived, and she was welcomed like a lost child. A few of the older staff remembered her mother's death. She'd never forgotten their kindness that had made the harsh, cruel days a little softer.

They ushered her inside. No, she wouldn't take coffee today, she said. She was only looking for her mother's necklace, which she thought she'd tucked away safely in her room. Yes, it was a shame her father wasn't here to see her. They all nodded, as if they understood. Though none of them could know the true extent of her suffering here.

Thea hurried up the stairs, her stomach cramping as she moved deeper into the house. Her nerves eased a little as she went into her room to fulfil the story she'd concocted. This space had been her one place of respite in the whole home, but still it oppressed her.

She fingered the necklace in her bag for reassurance. There was no time to dwell on the past. She had to move quickly to get out of this place.

Thea opened a few drawers and cupboards, to ensure the room looked searched, then set off down the hall for her father's study. On the way she passed Demetri's suite. The door was closed, but still a wave of nausea crippled her.

She stopped and leaned on the wall for a moment, regaining her composure. She was safe. He didn't live here anymore. But the memories had never left. The hair-pulling and tripping as a child, which had escalated to far worse. Her father never caring.

She swallowed and kept walking. She reached her father's study and slipped into the room. During those times he'd cut her off from the world she'd managed to sneak in and access the computer here. A poorly guarded thing, because her father thought himself impenetrable. She'd never looked for anything incriminating, only interested in getting messages to Elena and having some meagre contact with the outside world, but she felt sure there was something here that would help Christo.

Thea wiped clammy palms on her dress. She sat in the hard leather chair and fished a USB from her handbag. Switching on the computer, she waited until the lock screen appeared, asking for the password. Her father rarely changed it. When he did, in all his arrogance, he made it the name of his latest acquisition.

Her fingers trembled on the keyboard as she tried the last password—the name of his yacht, *Siren*. It failed. What could it be now? She took a few breaths to steady herself. There was time. His new mistress Athena? That might be it. Nothing. The date of her wedding? No. Her heartbeat spiked in panic. Atlas Shipping? Because she was sure her father coveted that too.

Nothing worked.

She pressed her palms to her eyes. She'd failed. Failed Christo. The realisation sat like a leaden weight in her stomach. What to do now?

She looked up, feeling small and ill. Like the little girl her father and Demetri had tried to defeat. Well, they wouldn't beat her. She cast her eyes around the room. Looked at all the treasures—those old, mouldering things Tito loved more than his living, breathing daughter. A new statue stood in the corner. Some bronzed sculpture of a Hindu god. She'd never seen it before. What if it hadn't been honestly purchased?

Thea shut down the computer, grabbed her phone from her bag and took a picture. *Artefacts.* She left the study and ran from room to room, snapping photographs of antiquities. It was a long shot, but the house was huge and there were rooms she hadn't explored since she was a child, many of them closed off. Now she opened every door, taking photos of what she could.

Finally she entered a small room she'd never seen before. It contained a desk and a bank of monitors, showing views from all areas of the house. A security room. She stared at the screens as if they might disclose some secrets. Show her a place she hadn't searched. They all flicked scratchily between different views except for one. It was fixed on the front door and drive.

And then she saw it. The sleek black car. A man getting out. Stopping briefly at the entrance. Looking up at the security camera for a second.

Demetri.

Thea froze. Then she ran.

* * *

Christo bounded up the stairs two at a time. Even in his jet it had been a gruelling flight after his tour of South East Asia's ports. Still, entering through the door of his home he felt seized with a burst of energy. He had news about Alexis.

Christo walked past his suite towards Thea's room, tearing at his tie and jacket on the way. He knocked on the door and opened it before there was any answer. Her scent permeated the air. Spice and honey. His heartbeat accelerated a notch. She hadn't made the space her own. It still looked like the guest suite she'd taken over. Clearly to her it was a temporary residence, one she'd leave soon enough.

He rubbed at the strange burning in his chest. He shouldn't be here. Not after giving the silent promise that he'd never touch her again. Though, to his shame, the horror of hurting her had subsided and his dreams were now plagued with visions of her golden skin and liquid amber eyes.

The memory of her perfume had sustained him through every smog-soaked city he'd visited. And on those lonely nights when he'd lain naked between expensive hotel sheets he'd burned to have her with him, head thrown back, gasping for breath as pleasure overwhelmed her.

He wouldn't act on any of it. But seeing her again—seeing her smile when he gave her the news about her brother—that was all the reward he needed.

Christo stalked downstairs, searching. Thea wasn't by the pool, lazing in the sunshine, showing off the slick honey-bronze skin he'd fantasised about too many times to count. Nor was she in her favourite place, at the table under a gnarled olive tree overhanging one of the more secluded terrace areas.

He'd joked that she hid from him there, and yet more often than not they'd both migrate to the dappled shade and drink coffee, whilst Thea tried to embarrass him in front of the staff with increasingly fanciful untruths.

He laughed—then stopped. Lies. Their whole liaison was built on them.

He looked up at the hazy sky peeking through green-grey leaves. Nothing here was based on truth but her naked body. Their soft, luscious kisses. They spoke of a truth all their own. And the way she'd screamed his name… There had been no lies there.

Something about her absence chastened him. She obviously didn't care when or if he returned. Nothing he wasn't used to. His parents had taught him well to have no expectations of being remembered. And, of course, it wasn't as if he'd left Thea a detailed itinerary. Part of his attempt to remind her that their relationship was a business arrangement.

Although his body didn't feel as if it was all business. He ached for her with a bone-deep hunger. Still, she could have found out about his return if she'd asked the right people. No, he'd clearly been harbouring vain hopes that she might have missed him. A ridiculous notion, and one he needed to overcome immediately.

He walked inside and checked the time. After a quick shower he could be back in his office, since there was nothing to keep him here.

As he walked towards the central stairs and his suite, he saw Anna.

She smiled. 'Mr Callas. Welcome home.'

He nodded as he passed her. 'Thank you.'

She'd probably know where Thea had gone, but it was none of his business. Still, he stopped and turned.

'Do you know where my wife is?'

A casual request. It would have been unusual if he *hadn't* asked. That was all.

'She's gone to her father's.'

Christo stilled. That wasn't a place she'd have travelled to willingly. His gut tightened.

'When?' The word came out sharper than he would have liked.

Anna frowned. 'An hour ago…maybe more?'

Hours? There was no prospect that she'd spend more

than minutes there. Had she been called over? She could be alone with that pig Demetri. Without anyone to protect her.

'Why did she go?'

'She said she had to find—'

'Has anyone heard from her? Or from Sergei?'

Christo tore the phone from his pocket and dialled the bodyguard's number. The phone rang. Nothing. He tried Thea. The same.

He looked back towards Anna. She blushed.

'Have I heard from Sergei? No...'

'From Thea? Please, it's important.'

'No. Nothing...'

Christo raked his hands through his hair, sucked in a steadying breath. He'd go to the Lambros home. Confront them. Get Thea back. If they'd touched her...

He swore.

'I'm leaving.'

Anna nodded. 'I'll call your driver.'

'No.'

He needed speed. As fast as his driver was, he'd take too much interest in Christo's safety. Christo didn't care about himself. All he wanted was to find Thea and bring her home. Protect her, as he'd promised.

'My keys. For the fastest car.'

'I don't know which—'

'Sports car. Black.'

'But all your cars are bl—'

There was no time for this. '*I'll* find them.'

If they'd hurt Thea he'd tear them apart, no matter the consequences. Christo clenched his fists. And if Sergei had allowed it to happen the man would never work again.

He calculated the time. It would take him twenty minutes to reach the house. And ten minutes to raze their world to the ground if they didn't tell him where she was.

His footsteps echoed against the walls. The door to the garage lay ahead.

Voices. He stopped. The door opened. *Thea.*

She walked through, sheathed in an inky black dress with her hair slicked back. Sergei followed her into the hall. His usually impassive face was cracked and worried.

Christo rushed forward, anger breaking like a wave on a reef. 'Did they hurt you?'

She looked up, her face pale and grey as moonlight. He caught her as she slumped into him.

'I need to go upstairs. Shower.'

Her voice was soft and fragile as a moth's wing. Christo swung her into his arms, where she clung. So light...so brittle. Like if he squeezed too hard she'd shatter.

He stalked past the staff, all their faces tinged with concern. The realisation hit him. They cared for her. Deeply. In the time she'd been with him she'd made her mark.

His jaw clenched as a strange thought came over him. This was how it should have been on their wedding night. Sweeping her into his arms. Carrying her upstairs to their room. Making love to her. *Loving* her. It should have been the happiest day of her life rather than what she'd actually had.

The guilt flooded over him, tainting him like a slick of oil. He needed to wash them both clean of it.

Christo carried her into his suite, set her down in the bathroom. A thready pulse flickered at the base of her throat. She stepped out of her shoes as he turned on the shower, scalding hot. Steam fogged the room.

'Why, Thea?'

She looked down at her feet and shook her head. He moved behind her and undid her zip, let the dress fall from her body. He unhooked her bra, slid her underwear down her legs till she stood there naked. He removed the pins from her tight bun and ran his fingers through her hair as it tumbled around her shoulders. He took off his watch, kicked off his shoes. Not caring that he was clothed, Christo walked her under the coursing water and held her close.

She trembled in his arms. Her skin was still cold even with the heat pounding it.

Christo took some soap, slicking it over her back and down her arms. He turned her around, checking for any sign she'd been hurt. She leaned forward, splaying her hands on the wall for support as he kept up his slow exploration.

It could almost have been worship as he knelt at her feet, looking up as the water sluiced down her spine through ribbons of dark hair. The light above shone like a halo over her head. He worked slowly. Massaged the taut, bunched muscles of her calves till they relaxed. Stroked the smooth skin of her thighs until she moaned, soft and long.

The sound punched his gut. Whatever haunted her, he'd wash her clean of it. Then he stood. His trousers were tight, the fine wool shrunken. Moving to her hair, he washed it, his nails scraping her scalp. Her head tipped back, her eyes closed, and mascara running down her cheeks in black streaks. He wiped away the last traces with a flannel.

When he was sure he'd washed off as much of the taint of the day as he could, he cast his ruined clothes aside. Turned off the scalding water and lashed a thick towel around his waist.

Then he grabbed a bathrobe from the back of the door and dressed her in it with care. In the oversized garment she looked tiny, vulnerable. He towelled her hair, swept her into his arms and carried her to the bed. The bed he'd sworn never to take her to again. But she needed him now.

He settled with her on the covers, cradling her as she nestled into him, female perfection in his arms. Her damp hair lay cool against his chest. He held her tight. She had to know she was safe. Here, with him.

And he asked the question again. 'Why did you go to your father's?'

There was nothing for a heartbeat, and then her slender shoulders rose and fell in a heavy sigh.

'I went there for you.'

CHAPTER THIRTEEN

No. *No.* SHE shouldn't have placed herself at risk. Not for him. He'd never have asked, knowing what he did now about her father and brother. To think she'd thrust herself in harm's way—and for what? There was nothing worth the price she might have paid.

'Thea. I'd *never* have asked you.'

'I know. But my father… Demetri. They won't let you go. They said they'd destroy you. I had to do something.'

He tightened his arms around her. In that moment he would have given her anything. Anything she wanted. 'I told you—Raul and I have enough.'

'I knew I could access the house. I thought maybe on the computers… I wanted to give you more.'

Christo tensed. He had strong circumstantial evidence. Enough for the authorities. But irrefutable proof… Surely it wasn't that easy?

'I tried, but couldn't figure out the password. He'd changed it.'

Christo relaxed. Of course. Nothing was ever easy for him. It didn't matter anyway—all he cared about was what had caused the fear he'd had to cleanse from her skin. Because if anyone had hurt her he'd chase them to the gates of Hades and cast them into its pits for eternity.

'What happened?'

'No one was supposed to be there. Then Demetri arrived. I couldn't avoid him.' Her voice cracked. 'I pretended I was looking for my mother's necklace. I'd taken it there. It was in my handbag. I showed it to him.'

He cradled her close. 'Did he believe you?'

'He said that my mother never changed her will. That my

father inherited everything so the necklace was his. Demetri snatched it away and kept it.' She shuddered.

That she'd risked herself for him, tore Christo's heart in two.

'I'll get it back. I promise you.'

She didn't seem to hear him, her voice broken and strained. 'It was worth nothing. A St Christopher medal. My mother gave it to me…said we would be travelling…it would keep us safe. She arranged to take me away one day. I waited in the kitchens by the door. Waited and waited and she didn't come. She was run down by a car in the street near the house. She was coming for me and she died.'

A tight curl of rage twisted in his chest. Demetri would not keep that heirloom from Thea. He had no right to it other than out of a belief driven by his own bitterness and hatred.

Christo began to move, but she held him tight.

'Don't leave me.'

He settled back into the covers. 'I won't.'

Right now, he'd give her whatever she asked. He kissed the top of her head. Her hair was now drying in a tangled mass. He ran his fingers through it to straighten it, easing out the knots. He still had information for her—some measure of happiness he could offer as part of his penance. The news from Raul.

'We've found Alexis.'

Thea stiffened in his arms. Then the sobbing began— heaving gulps with no control. Crying till his chest was soaked with her tears.

'He's been living rough, but Raul has him safe. It's better that you don't know where he is for now.'

'Thank you.'

The sobs subsided to a quiet weeping. He continued combing his fingers through the silken strands of her hair, smoothing them into a coffee-coloured river on his chest.

Trying to soothe the pain their marriage had caused her yet again.

'Raul can take a message to him. No other communication's wise until we deal with these false charges.'

Thea nodded, then spoke, her breath warm against his chest. 'I took pictures.' Her words scraped out, barely a whisper.

'Of what?'

Thea grew heavy against him, her limbs soft and supple. He ached to ease her onto her back. To caress her body till she wept from pleasure, not heartache. But he wouldn't take any more from her. He'd taken enough.

'The old things he loves better than me. The antiquities...'

And as Christo wrapped his arms around her he realised that she might have saved him after all.

A dull ache throbbed at Thea's temples. She'd handed her phone to Christo and told him to go. To download the photographs and send them to Raul. Not that she'd wanted him to leave. What she wanted was to kiss him until his lips and tongue erased the day from her body and soul. But all he'd do was hold her.

She must have slept. The shadows were now long. A golden glow filled the room. She rolled over in bed and saw him. A tall, dark shape in the doorway. She held out her hand. He walked in and took it, kissing her fingertips, the bed dipping as he sat on its edge.

'Did Raul find anything?'

'He'll search the lost antiquities registers. It'll take time.'

Christo brushed a stray lock of hair from her face. She closed her eyes and relished the stroke of his fingertips, her body liquefying at his touch. He was so solid. She felt no fear when he was close. Only a calm, dreamlike stillness. Like a drug to balm her anxious soul.

His finger ran along the edge of the collar of her robe,

following it to where it plunged between her breasts. 'Promise me something, Thea.'

His face was dark and serious. So beautiful. As she'd always imagined the embodiment of a god. Tall. Pure. Perfectly etched lines.

Her breath hitched as the gentle stroke of his fingers started through her hair. 'What?'

'Never take a risk for me again. It's not worth it.'

She touched her hand to the side of his face. It was what he hadn't said that spoke volumes. Christo had never been shown love as a child. He couldn't understand. *He* was worth it.

'Then don't leave me again,' she said.

He smiled, but only with his mouth. His eyes looked soft and sad. Her heart cracked. He continued stroking her. Gentle caresses that drove her to the edge of insanity. Her skin heated and prickled under the robe. An ache throbbed between her thighs. If only his hand would drift lower...trail burning fingertips down her abdomen to stoke the heat between her legs till they both caught fire and burned.

'I've taken enough. I won't have you trading your safety as well.'

She had a kernel of a thought—bright and bold. 'Are you saying you're indebted to me?'

'Yes.'

'Then I want—'

'Anything.'

'Make love to me.'

He stopped, and that was the cruellest torture of all. She'd combust right here if he didn't keep touching her. How could he have such control? Every nerve sang for him. Tight, shimmering and alive with his closeness.

'You said *anything*, Christo.'

The ghost of a smile played on his lips. 'I did.'

He leaned forward, placing his forearms on either side of her head. His nose touched hers, his breath caressing her cheek. He brushed his lips along the shell of her ear. Trailed kisses down her neck. She arched her back, a shiver of anticipation running through her. Her breath was coming in soft pants. Her hands worked at the tie of her robe.

'Patience,' he whispered. 'Lie still.'

She did as he asked. Waited.

The slow slide of his lips on her skin traced her jaw in languid kisses till he reached her mouth. His lips hovered above hers. She moaned. His mouth captured the sound, his tongue plundering as it joined hers in an erotic dance.

She wrapped her arms around his muscular torso, his back flexing and tense. His left hand moved to the tie of her robe and undid the knot in one swift pull, easing the fabric open so cool air washed over her. He cupped the underside of her left breast. Traced his fingers to the nipple which he rolled with exquisite care between his fingers.

An arrow of heat tore through her body, shocking between her legs. He skimmed a hand down her side and her thighs relaxed, moved apart. Inviting him.

'My beautiful wife...' he murmured.

She lay almost naked. He was fully clothed. The brush of his cotton shirt against her sensitive skin. The crisp smell of starch, the soft, smooth wool of his trousers. Her every nerve stood on end in anticipation. She squirmed and gasped and moaned at the suck and swipe of his tongue as he teased each nipple in turn.

'You want something? Hmm?'

The only sound she could utter was one of frustration. It had been over a week since his hands had been on her body. She was plump, ripe, desperate to be devoured.

Christo's tongue traced down her abdomen. He blew on the moist trail. Goose bumps bloomed on her overheated skin. He circled her navel and moved lower, then lower.

Thea held her breath. Waiting. He dipped between her legs, teasing softly. She gasped, almost leaping from the bed. He held her hips still.

'It's all for you.'

He slid his hands under her backside, cupping it, bringing her body to his mouth. His tongue explored with maddening precision. She raked her hands through his hair before gripping tight. Tried to hold him in place whilst the rest of her fought to escape the blinding sensation hitting her like lightning.

It was too much. The insistent stroke of his tongue. The crisp cotton where her legs touched his shirt. The stubble of his chin scratching the soft skin of her inner thigh as he feasted. Her world became the swirl of his tongue. The sparks of bright light flickering and shimmering behind her closed eyes. The noises she made. Breathy sounds, pleading for release as he taunted her with pleasure, taking her higher and higher till she was ready to soar, afraid to leap because it would ruin her.

He stopped for a second. She groaned in protest as a wicked smile played on his decadent lips.

'If I have to spend all night…' his breath toyed between her legs '…you'll come for me.'

She whimpered as a sheen of perspiration misted her skin. Her body trembled in fever and need till he dropped his head.

With one sharp, hard flick of his tongue she flew, screaming his name to the heavens.

'Christo!'

Only Christo.

CHAPTER FOURTEEN

THEA WASN'T SURE how to seduce a man. Particularly when said man was her husband. But if her own orgasms were any measure she was doing spectacularly well. Christo had denied her nothing. Using his body to pleasure her till she trembled and broke again and again, before falling into an exhausted sleep in his arms.

Sure, he'd had orgasms too. But he held something back, focused on her pleasure. She wanted to drive him as mindless as he did her. Crack the control he always seemed to hold on to like a shield.

Oh, he wanted her. Whenever she was near him his eyes coloured to the dark green of a hailstorm. His nostrils flared as she came close, right before he swept her into his arms and took her on another journey to ecstasy. And she could always feel him through his clothes. So hard and ready. But when she tried to take over and give him something with no thought for herself he didn't relent. Only whispering the words, *'It's all for you.'*

Well, tonight it was all for him. She knew a thing or two about control, and this was a battle she'd win.

She looked in the mirror and fluffed her hair till it hung messy and wanton. He liked it long and loose, so he could bury his hands in it as he held her tight for a searing kiss. She shivered. *No.* This was about Christo. His pleasure, not hers.

She smoothed her dress. Black. Fitted. The fabric soft and silky against her curves. She'd decided against a bra. A teardrop gold pendant hung low in her cleavage. She turned to look at the back. Saw the way it hugged her rounded backside. It was her least favourite feature. Though Christo seemed to love it, from the way he'd grab her and draw her close as they kissed.

Thea smiled over her shoulder. She had an idea... She bunched up her dress and shimmied out of her underwear. Nerves fluttered in her belly. *There*. He'd know the minute he touched her. She'd soon see if he could stop himself tonight. He'd lose himself in her. She'd ensure it.

She'd organised a candlelit meal on her favourite terrace. Secluded, peaceful. She reached the beautifully appointed table and took a glass of champagne to quell her nerves. She had no doubt Christo would make her mindless with pleasure, but could she do the same for him?

Best not to think too hard... Simply act. Touch, tease, tempt...

'Thea.'

She whipped around as the sound of his voice caressed down her spine. He tugged his tie through the collar of his shirt, winding it around his hand before tucking it in a pocket. Then he undid the two top buttons. She swallowed, her mouth dry.

'Have some champagne.'

She poured for him. As usual, he feasted on her with his gaze. Scorched her with a head-to-toe appraisal that had her wanting to shed her clothes and bare herself to him.

How could he do this to her? Needing this man had never been part of their arrangement. Yet the ferocity of her desire seemed as natural as breathing.

He took the glass she handed to him and placed it on the tabletop, drew her close. His lips were upon hers before she could think. His tongue explored her mouth greedily as his hands slid over her body. She turned liquid, her core aching.

He pulled back, an eyebrow quirked. 'Nothing under the dress?' He chuckled, a low and throaty sound that wound through her on a fiery journey. *'Koukla mou...'*

She'd taunted him in the past to say those words with feeling. Tonight they were rough and coated with desire. The way she'd dreamed of them being said. And the need in his voice punctuated every syllable.

She slid her arms around his neck and looked into his face. The hunger smouldering there almost cut her off at the knees.

'Have dinner with me,' she said. 'Let me take you to bed. Make love to you.'

'I thought that was what we'd been doing.'

'You know what I mean, Christo. You said you'd give me anything. Now I want to give you something in return.'

He brushed a lock of hair behind her ear and smiled. 'Ah, the demon that's been unleashed. My beautiful temptress. You should've been called Eve.'

'I want you.'

She dropped her hand between them and brushed it across the hard bulge in his groin. His breath hitched.

'I want *this*. One word and you'll have me on my knees, showing you how much.'

'Never kneel for me, Thea.'

Kneel for him? She'd worship him.

'You're worth more than you know.'

He hesitated, a look of something like uncertainty on his face. It was striking in a man she'd once thought was certain of everything.

'I'm not—'

'Shh...'

Thea placed a finger on his lips and stopped him. She wrapped her arms around his neck. He dragged her close and plundered her mouth. Drove her back till she hit the balustrade. His hand went to her left breast, teasing the nipple until it pinched and hardened through the soft fabric of her clothes.

She'd have him here. Now. Out under the stars. She didn't care who could see. She'd never get enough of this man.

He groaned her name. Hitched up the back of her dress and smoothed his large, warm palms over her bare buttocks. Slid a hand between her legs and stroked her.

'Wet. Perfect. Ready for me.'

'Always. *Please.*'

Thea gripped the front of his shirt, crushing the smooth white fabric. If he didn't do something soon she'd combust.

She fumbled with the front of his belt, trying to undo it.

'Protection…' he said.

'No time. Don't care.'

He took a step back and stilled her hands. 'We do have time. You should care.'

He couldn't do this to her again. She wanted to feel him naked against her. Hear him groan and shout her name as he found release, lost control, all because of her.

She stifled a sob. 'I need to be yours.'

Christo bundled her into his arms and whispered fiercely in her ear. 'We'll go to my suite, and I *will* use protection.' His thumbs grazed her nipples and she shivered. 'Then I am going to bend you over and take you so deeply you won't remember where you end and I begin. And you will *never* doubt that tonight you're mine.'

This wasn't going to plan, but she didn't care. Christo didn't believe her words, so she'd show it with her body. In bed, she'd prove how worthy he was.

He took her hand. They began walking towards the house. At the French doors leading inside he looked down at her tenderly. 'Should I carry you?'

Carry her over the threshold? The meaning loomed large. *Yes.*

But before she could answer Sergei rounded the corner with Anna. They stopped.

Christo glared at the interruption. 'What?'

Anna looked at her toes. Sergei merely stared straight ahead. When he spoke, his voice was impassive.

'Mr Callas. It's your father.'

If time could stand still, he'd have chosen hours ago. Out on the terrace with Thea's arms around his neck, her eyes burning into him. The words *'You're worth more than you know...'* on her lips.

But time had stopped here. In a darkened room, with an old man.

Christo sat in a chair by the bed. Wherever he'd gone now, at least his father looked peaceful. That was what the nurse had said. It had been a good death, whatever the hell that meant.

He'd sped here and he'd been too late. A private nurse had sat with him in his final moments. Laid him out. Christo didn't know how he felt about that. It was as if his insides were hollowed out. His skin and bones a mere shell around nothingness.

He stood and walked to the door. The nurse hovered outside. 'Once again, Mr Callas, I'm sorry.'

Christo nodded. 'My father did things in his own way and in his own time.'

'He left me a note to give you. For this moment.' She handed over a white envelope and placed a hand on his arm. 'It was my pleasure to look after him for you.'

She smiled. Patted him and walked away. Leaving Christo alone in the long hallway.

He strode out of the house as if death itself was chasing him. His chest heaved with the need for air. He burst out through the front door and bent at the waist, gasping for breath.

It was over. Time to go and start making arrangements. Try to maintain the lie of his father's legacy.

Christo slid into the car he'd parked at the front of his father's house and drove through the darkened streets. The whole world lay asleep, which was what he wanted to be too. Insensible to everything.

He drove through the gates of his home into the garage, where he sat for a moment. The white envelope taunted him from the passenger seat. He tore it open and read.

Dear Christo,
Now is a time to dwell on the living, not the dead...

There were instructions for the funeral. Who to invite, who to forbid. Advice on the allowance made for his mother, which would keep her in some style, but would not be enough to make either her or her lover happy. There was some talk about his joy at his son's marriage and his hope for grandchildren.

Hope. For a future which wasn't Christo's to have, not knowing how to love. Selfishness was the only lesson taught to him.

He crushed the empty envelope in his hand. Turning over the letter, he read the final page.

I know you won't grieve for me. That I was not much of a father.
I can't change how harshly I treated you, though the past is what made you the man you are now. But of all the hopes and regrets a foolish man has at the end, the one message that stays with me is this:
Never believe you weren't wanted.

What did that mean? He hadn't been wanted by his mother. She'd barely even acknowledged his existence once her future was secure. And as for his father—unloved by the wife who'd craved the money and not the man, searching for love again and again and in the process almost destroying Atlas.

The capacity to love didn't run in his parents' veins. Their blood had been passed to him.

And now he'd tried weaving Thea into his poisoned web of selfishness and subterfuge. He'd effectively held her captive. Then she'd offered to make love to him without protection. She had to know that meant the risk of pregnancy. That if she conceived their child there was no letting her go.

But now the reason to keep her had gone.

He dropped his head to the steering wheel. The gnawing ache of realisation filled him with endless torment.

He didn't know how long he sat there. Only that his muscles were stiff and the world was cold.

A shadow crossed the driver's window and the door cracked open.

'You can't stay here all night.'

Thea's voice was a soft caress on his wounded soul. She took his hand and led him through the darkened house to his room, where she peeled off his clothes, stripping him layer by layer. Then she lay down on his bed. Inviting him to her. Inviting him home.

He fell into her. This woman who gave and gave. But if she stayed too long he would take everything, leaving her a husk.

The leaden weight of the evening crushed him. He couldn't move. Wrapped in comforting arms which smoothed over his body, curling around him as if she was bandaging all the pain, he'd rest a while. Let the beautiful light of her soul illuminate all his dark places.

He still had time. Because just before his darkness extinguished her flame he would let her go.

CHAPTER FIFTEEN

A WEDDING. A FUNERAL. Christo knew what came next but had been putting off the inevitable. The will had been read, his mother's hysterics managed and the estate divided. There was no reason to cling to what couldn't be.

Coward.

He knotted his tie, tightening it like a noose around his neck. As he did so Thea rose from the bed naked and wrapped her body around his, wishing him a good day at work in the best possible way.

He slid his hand into her soft, warm hair. The silken strands held the exotic scent that was all her. He breathed her in. Each morning their ritual was the same. He'd get ready early, in the hope of leaving without seeing her, but something would always draw him back to the bedroom where they now spent every night. She'd ignited a hunger in him that wouldn't be sated.

Thea tipped her head back and smiled. 'Will you be home early tonight?' Her voice was husky, holding the promise of another indulgent evening.

How could he be in the presence of such a woman? This goddess like Aphrodite risen from the ocean? Someone who gave and gave, when all he wanted to do was take?

But he'd made her a promise. One he'd keep.

He had no knowledge of how to love. His parents had seen to that. Obsession? Yes. Sex? For sure. But Thea deserved more. Her youth and her life had been stolen from her by her father, her brother and now him. She deserved to *choose* a man to love—not be sold to the highest bidder for another's benefit. To be free from her cage. To have fun and go out, with her own money and resources.

That was what she'd planned and that was what he'd give

her. No matter how much the thought squeezed his heart till it almost stopped beating.

He dropped his mouth to hers and claimed it. Her lips were soft and drugging and she sighed, opening to him. His tongue slid in to taste her. Pure nectar. As sweet as honey. Her breathy sigh chased away all common sense as her body taunted and tempted him. He returned the kiss as if it was his last day on earth.

She moaned. 'Do you have to go to work at all?'

Yes. Today was his most important day. The day when he'd try to be the man Thea deserved.

She'd thank him. Maybe not now, but in the end.

'I have meetings. Don't wait up for me tonight.'

One more night with her and he might not do what needed to be done.

He pulled Thea in for a last, lingering kiss. The bright glow of her beauty warmed him. When he let her go that light would be gone. Darkness would take over again. It was what he knew, so he'd welcome it like an old friend. They could reacquaint themselves over a bottle of cognac in a lengthy future of lonely nights together.

He called his driver and left for his first and most important destination of the day.

The ostentation of the Lambros Bank's headquarters disgusted him. But it was where the story of Christo and Thea would end. When he'd called for a meeting Tito and Demetri had asked him to come here. No doubt they wanted to impress, to instil fear. It wouldn't work. He feared no one. Especially not these craven men. His only aim was to ensure that by the end of today Thea had everything she deserved.

He strode into the building and punched the lift button for the top floor. Their arrogance was laid out in front of him as the lift doors slid open on the pompous gilt and antiquities adorning the executive suite's foyer. There he sat in a cold leather chair. Waiting as he knew they'd make him.

He didn't care. It gave him a few more moments to cherish the gift of Thea. He twisted the wedding ring on his finger, felt the smooth gold warm under his touch. Still shiny and new. Witness to the privilege of being her husband. Of doing this for her.

'Mr Callas?' An immaculate blonde woman greeted him with a smiling mouth and unsmiling eyes. 'They'll see you now. Sincere apologies for the delay.'

There was nothing sincere about the look on her face. He followed her dismissive gesture through a wooden door into an office of cream marble and garish gold. Tito Lambros sat at a massive desk which looked as if it had been hewn from a solid piece of stone. As cold and hard as the man behind it. Demetri was perched on its front corner like a bird of prey waiting to strike. A large painting hung behind Tito, full of darkness and violence.

Christo raised an eyebrow. 'Jesus casting out the moneylenders. By El Greco, I believe?'

'I didn't know you had an interest in art,' Tito drawled.

Christo cocked his head, his voice full of menace. 'I've acquired an eye for hidden treasures.'

'As indeed this was. Locked away for centuries. A private collector found himself in some difficulty, so I helped. Or rather his sale of the painting to me did.'

'A strange picture for a banker to own...'

'You think? It's an attempt to get rid of us, and yet we're still here. It shows that in the end we always win.' Tito gave a slow and evil smile. 'I see it as a telling reminder to those who want to believe otherwise.'

Christo smiled back. Ah, the fall would be so sweet when it came...

He took a seat, without being invited.

'Once again, I'm sorry about your father,' Tito went on. 'Of course it means Atlas Shipping is now yours. To succeed with or fail. It would be a shame for my daughter if it were the latter.'

His daughter. Even now Tito hadn't relinquished her. That would change soon.

'Thea hasn't anything to fear from me.'

He'd failed her once. He would never fail her again.

He turned to Demetri. 'You took something of hers. A necklace her mother gave her. I want it back.'

'That cheap trinket?' His lips curled into a sneer. 'I misplaced it.'

'Then that carelessness will cost you,' Christo said, his voice sharp and cold as a steel blade.

'My son's only careless with meaningless things,' Tito said. 'Luckily I have it.'

He opened the drawer next to him, pulled out a slim gold chain with a pendant and tossed it across the desk. Christo caught it in one hand.

'But you didn't come for a necklace. Why are you here?'

Now the game would be played—a game he planned to win.

Christo slipped the pendant into his suit pocket and lounged back in his chair. 'You lied. Thea wasn't a willing partner in this marriage. I'm granting her a divorce.'

Demetri pushed himself up from the corner of his father's desk. 'That's not what was agreed. You owe my father.'

'Atlas Shipping owes your father's bank. Personally, I owe him nothing. Except contempt.'

'How dared you? That loan—'

Thea's father lifted two fingers and Demetri was silenced.

'That loan was a noose, designed to throttle me at the appropriate moment,' Christo said. 'But now Atlas's loan repayments are up to date. I rectified that oversight of my father's. And by the end of the week the loan will be repaid in full.'

Tito regarded Christo over steepled fingers. 'Paying back early means penalty interest—which you can't afford. It'll ruin you or take you close.'

Christo smiled blandly. 'You underestimate my abilities.'

'Perhaps... But you can't rectify all your father's mistakes. The antiquity smuggling, for one. If that's disclosed your ruination will be complete.'

Christo grinned. Tito Lambros had no idea how deep a mire he was wading into.

'I was hoping you'd come to that. My father left several letters before he died. One was to his solicitor, documenting what he knew about the stolen treasures he had unwittingly allowed Atlas to transport. Most interesting were his comments about *your* suspected involvement. And then there's your link to a particular ship's captain...'

A man who'd become suspiciously lax about documentation and the cargo that went onto each vessel. That was the information they'd sought from Thea, trying to weave her into their web of deceit. Getting more to blackmail her with when the need arose.

'I've terminated his services, if you're curious. Interpol want to talk to him.'

Tito sat back in his chair, his eyes darting to Demetri. 'Your father's letters won't be believed. They're the words of a dying man, bitterly regretting the errors he made, and trying to blame someone else for his folly.'

And this was where Thea's help had saved him—yet even now she didn't realise how much she'd done.

Christo took a long, slow breath, savouring the moment. 'Perhaps. But the authorities will be interested to see the security footage from that secret room you have in your house. If I sent it to the lost antiquities register what would they find?'

Demetri stared at his father, wide-eyed.

Tito paled.

Christo had them—and he wouldn't rest till they were finished. He stood, leaning forward and splaying his hands on the frigid marble of Tito's desk.

'All those times you locked Thea away, her only contact came from breaking into the computer in your office to speak to her friends. You may have changed your passwords there, but you forgot the passwords on your security system. It was only a matter of my consultants working through the list Thea gave me to find the right one. Apparently the hack isn't complicated if you know how.'

'You're lying.' Tito's voice came out hoarse and raw.

'You want to test that theory?'

The two men said nothing.

Christo smiled. 'Now, let's talk about the penalty interest…'

Two hours later Christo sauntered to his car. He slid into the back seat, took a folder from his briefcase and pulled out a sheaf of documents. Flicking through them, he came to Thea's signature on the back page. He traced a finger over the feminine writing, sitting there with pain embedded in him like a knife as he stared at the blank space where his own signature would go.

'Where to next, Mr Callas?' his driver asked.

He swallowed the agony down. Later he'd dwell. For now, he could never forget that everything he did was for her. All for her.

'To my lawyer's,' he said.

Christo slipped a pen out of the top pocket of his suit jacket. Scrawling his name on the line below Thea's, he did what he had promised all those months ago. He set her free.

CHAPTER SIXTEEN

THEA FINISHED HER morning coffee. Christo hadn't come for breakfast, and last night he hadn't graced their bed. She'd woken that morning to cold sheets where his warm body normally lay and she'd been struck by the realisation that even after one night apart she missed him. Missed his touch, the way it filled her with liquid heat, with something aching, trembling. Out of control.

She didn't know how she'd lived without it. In such a short time he'd become her every waking thought. Her night-time passion. Her secret addiction.

Should she look for him?

Thea knew he and Raul had been working long hours on the meagre information she'd given them. Trying to connect her father to something illegal and free Christo from Tito's clutches. Perhaps that was what he'd been doing last night.

Anyway, this morning there was no time to find him. She and Elena were going out together. Maybe to do some shopping now she could spend something of her own money rather than save for a grand escape. It would be fun for a change, and it was her time for a bit of fun. She hadn't thought about escaping for a long while.

She'd missed Elena desperately, thinking she and her friend would be separated permanently. Now the freedom to do normal things other women of her age did filled Thea with an almost girlish glee. For the first time in her life she felt valued. Cared for as an individual, not as a possession to be traded. Another thing to thank Christo for.

That list was ever increasing.

Thea smiled as she stretched in the morning sun, contemplating the number of ways she would thank her husband. A seductive pulse beat low in her belly...

As pleasant as it was, luxuriating in those thoughts, none of them would get her to Elena any faster. She sighed. Christo would have to wait.

Checking her watch, she made her way through the house, running into Anna.

'Thea—Mr Callas wants to see you. He's in his study.'

Thea grinned and her heart missed a few beats. She almost skipped to his office, not waiting to knock before she pushed the door open and walked in, snicking it shut behind her.

Christo sat at his massive oak desk. He clearly hadn't been home last night. The clothes he wore were the same as yesterday. His usually pristine shirt was crushed and his hair messed, as if he'd run his hand through it too many times. In most men it would look unkempt. In Christo it made him ruggedly handsome.

Thea's breath caught. The man could ignite her with a glance and she didn't care. The walls no longer closed in on her in quiet moments. She wasn't afraid of being trapped. Not anymore.

Christo raised tired eyes to hers. And there was something else she noticed. The lack of heat in them.

Every look he'd cast her way in the past weeks had threatened to singe her to ashes. Today there was nothing but... *devastation.*

Thea's heart pounded. Not even after his father had died had she seen him like this. Something terrible had happened.

'Christo, what's wrong?'

He motioned with his hand. 'Take a seat.'

So cool. Businesslike. It made her nervous.

She dropped into a solid leather chair opposite him. Leaned back. Crossed her legs. Tried to look casual and relaxed when inside she was bound in knots.

'I have to meet Elena soon.'

'This won't take long.'

His Adam's apple rose and fell as he swallowed. Her hands clenched reflexively into tight fists. The cut of her nails into her palms settled her racing heart a fraction.

'Is it about my father? Has Raul found anything?'

Christo shook his head. 'That wasn't a condition of granting what you wanted.'

His voice was so cold it chilled her bones.

He picked up a pen, tapped it on the leather desktop. 'You've fulfilled your obligations. That's all I ever required.'

She didn't understand. None of this made sense. 'What are you talking about?'

It was as if he wasn't looking at her, but at a point over her shoulder. She turned, the leather of her seat creaking under her, but there was no one there.

'Since Hector's gone and the estate's been settled, it's time to talk about bringing our arrangement to an end.'

She jerked back as if he'd slapped her. After what they'd shared... All their nights together... How could he do this now? Surely things had changed. How dared he do this without talking to her first about the future?

'You don't get to say that without looking me in the eyes.' She gritted her teeth. '*Look* at me, Christo.'

He didn't, instead leafing through some papers on his desk.

'How did you think it was going to end, Thea?'

She hadn't thought about an ending in such a long time. Now she understood the truth in her throbbing heart. She didn't know how she wanted it to end, only that she didn't want it to end immediately.

'As for your settlement,' he said, as if he was running through some awful shopping list, 'your investment's grown. That solar start-up in the States paid off. I've added half a million euros to the amount you had in the bank.'

Obviously Christo didn't feel the same way as her. Nothing had changed for him. She couldn't breathe. A tight band had wrapped around her chest.

'Christo. Please.' He was handing her everything she'd ever dreamed of and yet she wanted none of it.

'Ours was only ever a short-term arrangement. You wanted a life. I'm granting it to you. Along with a fully furnished house in Glyfada.'

At the beach? She loved the beach. But it was just another possession. Another *thing*. She wanted to hurl it right back at him.

'Is this what you want?' she asked.

He looked at her now, and all she saw was blankness. Nothing but the cold, dark heart of him. The man from the night of her marriage, from the negotiations with her father. Where was the gentle, passionate person she thought she'd discovered? It was as if he'd never existed.

Christo gave a curt nod. 'I signed the divorce papers yesterday and delivered them to my lawyer. It's done.'

'No!'

'There are no happily-ever-afters here,' he said, lifting the papers he'd been looking through and tapping them on the desktop till they were straight.

He put them in a folder and slid it across to her.

'In addition to those settlements I've negotiated a ten-million-euro payment from your father. You'll be a wealthy woman. Free to do whatever you want. The removal company will come tomorrow to pack your things. I've taken the liberty of delivering your motorcycle to your new home. I'll leave all the necessary keys with Anna. The estate agent will show you around.'

She didn't know this man. The man who stuck a knife in her heart with no remorse. There was nothing left of the husband who'd made love to her till she'd wept from pleasure. This man only caused pain.

'You've been busy.'

He was casting her out. Moving on. Had these past months meant nothing to him?

'You've kept me from the business I have to attend to. You wanted a life. I want my life back.'

The thought of him taking back his life made her ill. Living without her, seeing other women... She swallowed down the saliva flooding her mouth. Swallowed past the tight, choking feeling that crept into her throat, as if the world was trying to throttle her. He'd planned this all along, using her in the process. Well, she wouldn't let him see her humiliation.

'The wedding and engagement rings are yours to keep,' he said.

She looked at the still twinkling gems on her finger. Funny how she'd forgotten they were even there, and yet they were mocking her now. She wrenched them from her hand and tossed them on the leather desktop. Christo watched their trajectory as they bounced and fell in front of him.

'Since I'm not married any more I don't want them,' she hissed. 'Give them to your next bride of convenience.'

He shrugged, then stood and walked out from behind the desk. 'Your father has retracted his complaint against Alexis. He says it was an accounting error. The charges are in the process of being dropped. When that's happened, Raul will give you Alexis's new number.'

She slumped in the chair. At least some good had come from this disaster.

Christo stopped as he reached her. Sliding his hand into his pocket, he placed something carefully on the desktop. Thea saw the gleaming gold of her mother's necklace. She picked it up. The metal was warm from his hand. Tears pricked her eyes, burned her nose as she blinked hard.

She didn't look back as Christo walked away from her, as the door of his office clicked open. She felt his hesitation, heard the scuff of leather soles on carpet.

'Goodbye, Thea.'

The door closed behind him and he was gone from her life for ever.

CHAPTER SEVENTEEN

THEA TOYED WITH her lunch, chasing a rogue olive around the plate. Another meal. Another hour passing in this, the eighty-seventh day since she'd walked from Christo's home with everything and nothing.

Not that she'd been counting since that moment. Not at all. Not since those awful minutes when she'd left his office and a distraught Anna had handed her a bunch of keys and an envelope. No, it was done now.

She sipped at a glass of wine, which could have been vinegar for all she cared. Today her mission was to choose a gown for a function at the American Embassy in a few days' time. She was having fun. It was what she'd always wanted. It should have been perfect. No, it *was* perfect. It was…

'Are you missing Alexis?' Elena sat opposite, her lunch long devoured. She peered at Thea over a pair of oversized sunglasses.

A week earlier Alexis had left for Australia to visit his father. And, yes, she missed him. Their reunion had been full of joy and hugs and tears, and it hadn't been long enough after everything that had happened. Now he was spending six months travelling the world, and when he returned to Greece he was taking up a role in Raul's security company. She suspected that was Christo's doing too…

'*Paidi mou.* You're not happy.'

Wasn't she happy? She had everything she'd ever desired. A house. Wealth. Freedom. And what she *didn't* want—her father's money—she'd put to good use in funding a refuge for women who were escaping family violence. Achieving something worthwhile.

She had a wide circle of acquaintances. Her life was hers to control. All the freedom she'd ever wanted and yet those old fears returned late at night. Of being trapped in a cage. Rattling the bars till cold sweat prickled down her neck. The same fear which once had her clenching her fists till her nails bit into her palms.

Now those fears took her out early, riding her motorcycle in the predawn air. Riding till the sun rose. Pretending she could fly. Always pretending…

Elena reached out and squeezed her hand. 'What happened, Thea?'

Why did she feel so rooted to the ground when she could do anything she wanted?

Thea stared into her empty glass.

Christo.

She'd hated him in those days after she'd left his home. In those lonely days when she'd forgotten the words he'd repeated so often. *'It's all for you.'* Now, everywhere she turned, that was all she heard. His voice, whispering that truth in her ear.

When she'd walked into the exquisite house he'd chosen for her…when she'd waved Alexis away at the airport… when she'd heard the rumour that Demetri had betrayed her father to the authorities to save himself.

Christo had given it all to her. Everything she craved. Almost. But the most important part was missing. Leaving an ache which hadn't eased.

Thea looked up at her friend.

'I fell in love.'

Those simple words freed her. She smiled at the power of her admission. Felt a spark telling her that if she acknowledged that truth, anything was possible.

'I love Christo.'

Elena slapped her thigh. 'I knew it! So what are you going to do about it?'

Thea flopped in her seat. She had no answers. Did Christo love her in return? He'd loved her body—there she had no doubts. As for the rest…she didn't know. Their last conversation had left her questioning everything, hearing the chill in his voice as he froze her out of his life. But his actions... His desolation when he'd let her go...

Because in the end everything he'd done had all been for her. She couldn't sit back ignoring the truth any longer. She loved him. She wanted him. And moping about it was not an acceptable option.

'I've got to go.'

She stood, bumping the table as she rose. Her wine glass teetered. She steadied it.

Elena raised her eyebrows. 'Where?'

There was only one thing to do. Her first real choice. No more pretending.

'To tell Christo I love him.'

Thea rode her motorcycle through the open gates of Christo's mansion, pulling to a stop near the immense pots overflowing with the magenta riot of bougainvillea. As she removed her helmet the cast-iron gates behind her slid to a close. She tried to ignore the ominous clang as they locked.

Swinging from her seat, she stuffed her gloves into the helmet and hung it from the handlebars. Everything would be fine.

Tell that to her terrified heart.

She stopped and took a few deep breaths, catching the scent of citrus blossom drifting on the warm air, reminding her of a day when all she'd wanted to do was run. Well, she wasn't running away now. Instead, she strode to the front door, which opened as she reached it.

Anna.

Thea pulled her into a tight hug. 'I hope I haven't made things difficult for you by coming?'

'As I said when you called, you're worth the trouble. Anyway, nothing could make things more difficult than they are now.'

Anna led her into the bright foyer and closed the door behind them.

Thea unzipped her jacket, the cool air of the house washing over her. 'If anything happens today, you'll always have a job with me.'

Anna waved her hand, a tightness pinching her eyes. 'I'm not worried about my job… I'm hoping you can help Mr Callas.'

At his name, Thea felt a shock of adrenalin spike through her.

'How is he?'

'Unforgiving. Of himself, mostly. But there's more. Your room…he got rid of all the furniture. Curtains. Tore up the carpet. It's all bare. He refuses to allow us to speak of you. It's like you were never here.'

Thea's stomach heaved, pain knifing her deep inside. Did he really want her out of his life so badly? Maybe it had been a mistake coming here. Her hands curled into fists, the nails cutting into her palms. *No.* Fear wasn't going to win. She wouldn't run from this.

Thea flexed her fingers. 'Take me to him.'

Anna gave a tight smile. 'He's shut in his office—as usual.'

They walked in silence up the stairs. Past the magnificent paintings she'd first seen all those months ago. Then, this place had pressed in on her like a prison. Now, a feeling of calm washed over her. She'd come home—if only Christo would see that too.

Anna glanced back at Thea as they stood outside his closed door. She mouthed *Good luck*, then turned back and knocked.

'Come.'

That voice. Stern and uncompromising, it slid through her like fire in her blood. Her body trembled—but not from fear. From the agony of being away from this man for so long.

Anna opened the door and Thea slid past her, not giving Christo any time. He looked up at her, his eyes blank. Then confused. Then—

'What the hell are you doing here? Anna!'

The door had already snicked shut. Anna had sensibly gone.

'Don't blame her. I can be very persuasive when I want.'

He unfurled from his chair. All muscle and towering height. Funny, she'd never been intimidated by that. She noticed his clothes hung slightly looser. His trousers a touch lower on his hips. He wore a business shirt, top buttons open. Lean. Hungry. Predatory.

He canted forward, palms on the desktop. 'Answer my question.'

Oh, he'd give her nothing. She'd have to work hard for everything today.

She loosened the tie in her hair. Ruffled her hands through its long waves, flattened by her helmet. He watched, those green eyes tracing its fall over her shoulders, moving down to the split of her unzipped jacket, her heavy studded belt, to her boots and back.

When his eyes met hers again they were wild and dark. She smiled. 'You offered me my rings. I didn't want them then, but I do now.'

He stood back and his shoulders dropped. What was that look on his face now? Like a cloud passing over the sun? It could have been relief or disappointment. He turned towards the safe hidden in a cupboard behind his desk. She saw nothing but the broad expanse of his shoulders, narrow hips, standing stiff and severe.

'You should have called…' Christo's voice scored down her spine, rough as fingernails.

'I was told you were unlikely to speak to me.'

'You could have left a message.'

'It was the right time to visit.'

The safe cracked open. He withdrew a box, turned and placed it on the desk in front of him.

'I shouldn't be surprised. You said you liked shiny things.'

She shrugged. 'Being a young, single millionairess, it's all about the sparkle.'

'You don't need those to do that.' He nodded to the box. 'You're the belle of every ball.'

A glimmer of hope lit deep inside. She raised her eyebrows. 'Keeping an eye on me?'

'People say things…' Christo's throat worked as he swallowed. He shook his head. 'You have what you came for.'

No, she hadn't. Not yet.

She wiggled her fingers. 'I should put them on. Would you do the honours?'

He stared at her outstretched hand. The white line her rings had left was only recently faded.

His lips narrowed. 'What's this game?'

'No game. Not afraid of a few diamonds, are you?'

Christo grabbed the box, wrenched it open and snatched out the rings. He stalked round to her. 'They mean nothing,' he said as he reached for her hand. 'Not now.'

His fingers shook as he slid the rings onto hers. Once they were in place he snapped back as if he'd been burned. Oh, Christo. So strong. So hard. Denying himself what he truly wanted.

Thea held up her hand and looked at the glistening gems. They appeared to be newly cleaned.

'That feels better. You didn't do that before. Put the engagement ring on my finger.'

They were close now. She could see the rapid rise and fall of his chest as he breathed hard, the throbbing pulse at his throat.

'There was nothing romantic about our arrangement.'

She smiled and his eyes dropped to her mouth. His lips parted, then closed. He still desired her, but out of some misplaced nobility he believed that what he'd done was right. It was time to prove how wrong he was.

'I know your secret. You're a romantic man at heart. You crave it, if only you'd admit that to yourself.'

'You misunderstand me. I gave you everything you wanted. Go.'

His words were a plea, wounded and raw. And at his pain her bright, blinding love for him burst inside.

'You gave me money. I want something more.'

'There's nothing for you here.'

'Everything's here. I've come for your heart.'

Thea dropped to her knees in front of him. Looking up, she took his hands in hers.

'Because I love you with all of mine.'

Christo watched her kneel before him. All sorts of visions flickered through his head. Of dark nights, a warm bed and Thea. Always Thea. He'd attempted to exorcise the house of her short existence there, but even after removing everything from her room the ghost of her still haunted it. Her smell, her shadow was everywhere. Turning every day into a prison, a purgatory from which there was no escape.

'What madness is this?'

His voiced grated out, raw and ragged. He tried to pull his hands away but she held firm, gazing up at him with her cognac eyes. That look slid inside his veins. His one true addiction was setting him alight.

'Courage, Christo.'

He stilled. Courage? He was looking at the bravest person he knew. Him…? He was the coward who'd driven her to this. On her knees, begging him. The guilt of it clawed in his chest.

'You wanted your freedom,' he said.

Still she held tight. The heat of her infernal fingers scorched him. The light in her eyes reached into his dark places. Damn her. It would take him an age to recover from this.

'You touched me and I discovered what freedom was. It's inside myself, not outside the walls which surrounded me. It's loving with all that I am and all that I have. I'm free with *you*.'

When he looked at her face he saw it shining from within. Love. It poured from her and into him. How could she feel this way when he had nothing to give? And yet the pain of her absence cut through him.

He fell to his knees in front of her. 'I told you never to kneel. You should kneel to no man.'

'I'm not kneeling to *any* man. I'm kneeling to the man I love. The man with whom I want to spend the rest of my life. For better. For worse. Though I can't imagine anything worse than the pain of this time without you.'

'What are you asking?'

'Marry me.'

Time stopped. In this room, on his knees, looking into the soul of the woman he now knew he'd loved for months. She was handing him her heart. Did he have the courage to accept it and honour her the way he should?

'I don't know that I'm worthy.'

'You prove yourself worthy every day. I see it. Your staff see it. The only person who doesn't believe is you. So answer my question.'

He cupped her face in his hands. This incredible woman. He'd give her anything to ensure her happiness. Even his cracked and broken self. Because she wanted him. Believed in him.

He'd punished himself enough over the years, absorbing his parents' disapprobation. But why accept their opinions about him when he rejected their judgement on everything else? Perhaps he did deserve the love Thea showed him now.

There was only one way to find out.

'*I zoí mou, s'agapó.* My life, I love you.'

He'd fight every day to keep that smile on her face. He stood, pulling her with him. Holding her tight. Accepting all she offered.

'Yes. Was there any doubt of my answer?'

She nuzzled into his chest. 'Life's full of doubt. But I see you like you saw me. Only a man who truly loved me would have let me go.'

And only a woman who truly loved him would have asked for him back.

'My brave, beautiful Thea.'

'I must be brave. It seems I have a wedding to plan.'

She ran her hands through his hair and all he could think about was the bedroom down the hall and staying there for days.

No, she deserved more.

He grabbed his phone and called the harbour master. 'Yanis—ready the yacht. I'm travelling tomorrow. First light. With my fiancée.'

Thea raised her eyebrows.

'You can plan the wedding,' he said, 'but I intend to start the honeymoon early.'

He swung her into his arms and she squealed with laughter. 'I was right when I said you were a romantic.'

'It's all for you, Thea,' he murmured, brushing his lips across hers.

She cupped his face in her hands. 'No, not for me. From now on it's for *us*.'

He smiled at this woman who would hold his heart for ever.

'Always.'

EPILOGUE

WHITE MUSLIN CURTAINS billowed in the warm breeze from the Aegean. Each time they parted Christo caught a glimpse of the azure blue sea surrounding their island. Exquisite, but nothing matched the woman sprawled with him, replete on the rumpled sheets. Her bare skin like honey against the crisp white cotton.

Their trip here had been an escape after visiting Maria's grave on Karpathos. Tidying the space, leaving flowers. For him, comforting his wife. Such a strong woman Maria had borne in Thea, it left him in awe. That day at the cemetery Christo gave a silent word of thanks to the mother-in-law he'd never known, for giving him such an incredible young woman to cherish.

Six months on from their honeymoon on this island, and he was still immersed in the fulfilment of every day. The magnificent whitewashed mansion had become their haven and escape where they relived their renewed vows and commitment to one another. With Raul and Elena as witnesses, it was all they'd needed, standing barefoot on the golden sand here and declaring their love. Nothing more, nothing less.

There was a rustle beside him. He remained still, lying on his stomach as Thea sat up. She leaned across his body, her long hair trailing over his back sending goose bumps of pleasure shivering across his skin. Her warm breath ghosted over his right shoulder blade, before she dropped her mouth in a gentle kiss. Right over where he now had his own tattoo, of a bluebird like hers.

'Did it hurt?'

'You've asked me this before.' He felt her smile against his skin. 'Many times.' And each time he answered with the truth, she'd kiss *all* of him better. Inflicting her own kind of agony with her lips and hands. Now, it was his turn to smile. She bent down and kissed the upturned corner of his mouth.

'Tell me again,' she murmured, tracing the tattoo's outline with her clever fingers. He closed his eyes, allowing her to explore for a while, even though his body had other ideas which involved him being far more assertive, and preferably inside of her.

'Excessively.' He'd wanted to experience a little of what she'd gone through. Anyhow, the pain had been worth it to honour Thea, and nothing compared to her past hardships. It was also a reminder of what bound them together. The bluebird a symbol of joy, not suffering.

There'd be no more suffering, not if he could help it.

'My darling, brave husband.'

'I'm hardly brave.' He shrugged. 'My wife leaves me in her shadow.'

'You have your own fine attributes.'

Christo looked over his shoulder and raised an eyebrow. 'Well endowed?'

Thea tossed back her head, hair tumbling in unruly waves over her glorious, naked torso. Her throaty laugh sending a lick of pleasure right through him. It was his mission to hear it every day, because of him. He made sure she laughed loud and often. How he loved the sound.

'Now you're digging for compliments,' she said, the laughter warming her voice. 'When you know the answer to that question.'

Her skin flushed a beautiful pink. She'd perfected the art of looking seductive and coy all at once, and it never failed to intoxicate him. Their lovemaking left Christo in a constant state of deep, bone-numbing satisfaction. But it wasn't only in bed that his life had reached the status of perfection. It was in the day-to-day. A true partnership of hearts and minds. The simple things like cooking a meal together. Helping raise money for her women's refuge. Choosing colours for a nursery which wasn't needed yet, although they'd talked of children. Thea assured him it was good to be prepared and he relished her joy in the task. Who knew there were so many different shades of yellow? He'd come to learn them all.

Having her in his life and in his arms completed him in ways he'd never thought possible. The ultimate privilege. Anything seemed achievable, because of her. 'Now you're being elusive about my attributes.'

'Well,' she said, looking up at the ceiling as if thinking hard. Nibbling on her plump lower lip in a way which heated his blood. He shifted on the mattress, rolling onto his back. 'My husband's protective.'

'About you, of course.'

'And dogged.'

'Mmm…' His pursuit of her father and brother had been relentless and deserved. He wouldn't lower himself to even mentioning them in Thea's presence any more. The legal tangle they were mired in over stolen antiquities filled enough newspapers. The scandal complete. If Thea chose to read about what befell them, that was up to her. He hoped she forgot they'd ever existed.

'You're modest too,' she said. A smile of amusement hinted on her lips. He'd kiss that smile away soon enough. Christo stroked his fingers lazily over the skin of her thigh, her own responding goose bumps teasing his fingertips.

'Now my wife exaggerates.'

He sat up and wrestled a giggling Thea underneath him, before her body melted soft and pliant on the cool sheets. She wrapped her arms round his neck, threading her fingers into his hair. 'You're loving.' Her eyes gleamed the rich fire of cognac in candlelight. 'And lovable. Never forget that.'

How could he, when they told each other each day? When they showed it with their bodies and hearts and souls. He believed it now, the ghosts of his childhood well and truly exorcised.

'I'm loved.' He brushed his lips across hers as she drew him into a kiss. 'I love you.'

And Christo relished the lifetime of days ahead, to show Thea exactly how much.

* * * * *